W9-AUD-767

Death

of a

Kleptomaniac

ALSO BY KRISTEN TRACY

A Field Guide for Heartbreakers

Sharks & Boys

Death of a Kleptomaniac

Kristen Tracy

NEW YORK

FOR SARA CROWE, MY AGENT AND FRIEND
THANK YOU, THANK YOU, THANK YOU

First Edition
1 3 5 7 9 10 8 6 4 2
G475-5664-12252

Printed in the United States of America

Library of Congress Cataloging-in-Publication Data
Tracy, Kristen, 1972–
Death of a kleptomaniac/Kristen Tracy.—1st ed.
p. cm.
Summary: A sixteen-year-old girl with the uncontrollable urge to steal
is trapped in limbo with three days before her funeral to find redemption
and true love.
ISBN 978-1-4231-2752-9
[1. Dead—Fiction. 2. Future life—Fiction. 3. Coming of age—Fiction.
4. Love—Fiction.] I. Title.
PZ7.T68295De 2012
[Fic]—dc23 2011045659

Text is set in 11.5-point Sabon

Reinforced binding

Visit www.un-requiredreading.com

Let me fall
in love one last time, I beg them.
Teach me mortality, frighten me
into the present.

—Jack Gilbert

one

*B*ecause I am young, industrious, and mildly horny, I am capable of thinking multiple thoughts at the same time.

Thought One: Right before I kiss a guy, I experience obvious epiphanies.

Thought Two: I'm not cultured enough for Henry Shaw; he plays the saxophone.

Thought Three: If I add one more guy to my Junior Year Crush List, I'll reach unsustainable numbers before November.

Thought Four: Excluding people who come from old money and the East Coast, I *am* a fairly cultured person.

Thought Five: This is the first time I've ever listened to John Coltrane and known that I was listening to John Coltrane.

Thought Six: Henry wants to kiss me. I want to kiss Henry. Do it.

Thought Seven: Henry is dating Melka. Wait for Melka

to return to the Czech Republic. I am not a relationship wrecker.

Thought Eight: Kiss him. *Kiss him.*

My mind never stops. As I sit on Henry Shaw's well-vacuumed shag carpet, I run my hands through it, as if I'm petting a dog. Even though I've known Henry since fourth grade, this is the first time I've ever been in his room. It's no typical guy cave. It's clean, spacious, painted a neutral walnut color, well decorated, and I like his floor lamps. Backlit, Henry holds his saxophone with both hands and leans his head forward a little, cheeks inflated. How come I've never noticed the sexual nature of the saxophone before? Henry plays it with his whole body. And I feel the music come out of Henry with my whole body. When I close my eyes, I try to stop thinking. I spend too much time in my head. Henry and Melka. Henry and Melka. I won't bust up a relationship. It's not my style.

Henry pulls the horn from his mouth and sets down the instrument in a stand beside his bed.

"It's soulful," I say, hoping that a saxophone player will find that comment deep enough. Then I stop talking. Most of what I know about dating comes from cable television. And it's a well-dramatized fact that speaking the wrong words during key romantic junctures can derail all progress.

"Thanks," Henry says.

He looks sad as he sits down next to me on the carpet. We're supposed to be studying in the kitchen. We're not supposed to be alone in Henry's bedroom with the door shut. This isn't my normal. Kissing aside, I've only *really* made out with one guy, and it was in a car, because, due to my mildly horny predisposition, I try to avoid situations where I can become easily horizontal on surfaces that encourage coupling.

"You're so quiet," I say. But he's always quiet. I'm not saying anything beyond what our entire high school knows.

"I'm thinking about Melka," he says.

"Oh, God." I didn't mean to say that out loud. As casually as I can, I grab my right wrist with my left hand and feel for my pulse. It's a tactic I use to calm myself. It never occurred to me until this very moment that this might look weird.

"So you've heard," he says.

I let go of my wrist and shake my head. I feel like he's referring to a specific event. I stare into his face, into his eyes. They are so sad. He takes his glasses off so I can look directly at him. No glass barrier. Corny and inconvenient as it sounds, I'm getting lost in the eyes of Henry Shaw, an already-taken high school band geek. And on a school night! This is so impractical. I'm losing myself somewhere between Henry's black pupils and hazel irises. It's amazing that you can know someone for years and years and suddenly they can look so different, so *sexy*. He blinks and then I blink and then we both keep staring.

He finally speaks. "I broke up with Melka."

I swallow. And continue to stare.

"Oh," I say. Sounding so sorry, even though I'm not.

"It wasn't going anywhere," he says.

We're in high school. He was dating an exchange student. Where was he expecting it to go? But I don't say that. I blink. I say something that I think he might want to hear. "It has to be going somewhere."

His face moves closer to mine, and when I sense his breath approaching my mouth, I close my eyes. At the beginning of summer I made a promise that I would not waste my junior year. Everything I did had to matter. Because high school is important. This, I'd decided, was the year I was going to make my mark.

Henry laughs. I open my eyes.

"You're laughing at me?" I ask.

"It's your face," he says.

He's laughing at my face?

"You look cute when you close your eyes," he says.

I swat his leg pretty hard. I meant the strike to be flirtatious. But I hit him with a little too much enthusiasm.

"Do you want to stop?" he asks.

But we haven't started, I think.

"Do *you* want to stop?" I ask.

He stands up, and my whole body floods with disappointment.

"What kind of music do you like?" He walks to his desk, opens his laptop, and clicks through files.

"I'm new to jazz," I say.

He turns around and wags his finger at me like he's disappointed. "You're missing out. You want to hear Lee Konitz?"

I nod. Henry's right. I suddenly feel like I'm missing out

4

on everything. Why aren't we making out right now? Why haven't we been hooking up and listening to jazz from the very beginning? I guess fourth grade is a little young for that. When does a person even start playing the saxophone?

"Maybe you want to hear Jackie McLean?"

I nod again. "Both of them," I say. No more missing out.

While his back is to me, I lift a low-hanging sheet so I can peek under his bed. I glimpse a flash drive. A sock. Then I see a pair of keys strung together with a piece of yellow yarn. No dust. Henry is a clean guy. I reach under the bed and snag the keys. I settle the sheet back in place. I do this before he turns around. The keys slide easily into my front pocket and I'm excited in a different way.

"You like this?" he asks.

I nod again, and he sits down next to me. His thin body feels strong as he pulls me toward his lap. He runs his hands through my hair over and over again, and we just keep staring at each other. This is young love, I think. It's not supposed to make sense. It's supposed to unfold just like this in a bedroom where you were never supposed to be.

We lean toward each other until his lips touch my lips. After three gentle presses I feel his tongue. Four minutes ago I could never do this because Henry was dating Melka and he was not on my Crush List. Now I know what his tongue tastes like. He pulls away from my mouth, and my eyes pop open. Why did we stop kissing? We should never stop. We're just looking at each other. Watching each other breathe. I keep my head tilted and lips relaxed, hoping he'll lean forward and we'll start again. And then he does.

This time we aren't as gentle. We kiss desperately. Like it's a life-sustaining activity. My mind keeps trying to think. But I don't want to think.

Fast. Fast. Fast. His hands reach around my waist. They want to tug at my shirt. I can feel that they want to do that. But he doesn't let his hands go anywhere under my clothes. His fingers crawl along my back. We kiss. We kiss. His mouth is on my neck. We begin falling backward into a horizontal position. *Bad idea. Stay sitting up.* But then the base of a brass floor lamp is next to my head.

The sounds of songs I've never heard, instruments I can't identify, float out of the speakers on Henry's shelf. Then I hear his front door slam shut. Parents. The wall holding his band plaques shakes, and we fly apart. I lift myself until I'm on my knees, swooning from the best make-out session of my life.

"I'm supposed to be in your kitchen!" I whisper, panicked and a little dazed.

"You look so guilty," Henry says. "It's okay."

"Kitchen!" I whisper again, standing up, urgently making my way through the hallway, down the stairs. I need to prepare myself to say normal things to his mother. Or father. Or priest. Or whomever I encounter near the fake fruit bowl set out on the dining room table. I round the corner to the kitchen and am stunned to see somebody I know.

"Melka!" I say. Her blond hair is swept into a messy ponytail. Her face is a diamond of petite and well-placed bones; she's the tiniest girl at our school.

"Molly Weller?" Melka says. The way she utters my name makes it sound like a criminal act.

I don't say anything else. I react internally. *Henry gave his girlfriend-of-three-months keys to his house? Weird.*

"Dis? Dis? Is how you treat me?" Melka asks. Her eyes squint and tears gather in their corners. "You git wit Molly Weller?"

When she speaks my name the second time, she sounds disgusted.

"We were studying," I lie. "I've got to go."

"Melka, why are you here?" Henry asks. He looks beyond uncomfortable. "We're broken up."

I think he said that last bit of information for my benefit.

"Yesterday," Melka says. Her tears have intensified and turned toward sobbing.

I know I said I was leaving, but I continue to stand there. Maybe out of shock. Or possibly curiosity. Could what just happened be nothing more than a rebound? Is Henry like that?

"I left keys to my bike lock," Melka says. "Maybe in your room."

Henry nods. "Okay. You can go look. I haven't seen any keys. I'll go with you."

"Bye!" I say, racing to leave. Ugh. This feels so weird. They broke up yesterday and I'm making out with him today? Again, that's not my normal. I hurry down the sidewalk to my car. I pull open the door and sit. Through a lit window I see two figures. It's easy to tell Melka apart from Henry. Melka wants him back. She keeps moving her

7

super-slim figure closer and closer to him. I wonder what they're saying. I wish I could know. He looks so stiff. Even from their silhouettes it's pretty obvious that Henry doesn't like Melka anymore. Henry likes me. And I like Henry.

I mean, I think I do. What about Tate? We have our first date this weekend. I start my car. The year of making my mark is beginning to feel a little complicated. I can't like two guys at the same time. Can I? I peel out of Henry's driveway and turn on my headlights. As part of his annual car safety routine, my father recently replaced both bulbs, and I can tell. They illuminate the suburban roadway in front of me with two perfect cones of light. Henry or Tate? I notice the signal turning red just in time to ease to a comfortable stop. A woman with a backseat filled with grocery bags pulls up alongside me, and I smile at her. Melka will never find her keys. Why don't I feel worse about taking them?

The light turns green and I punch the accelerator. There is nothing wrong with liking two guys. I wanted Melka's keys. So I took Melka's keys. It happens. I have a big heart. I'm capable of liking lots of people. So what? And sometimes I take things. It's not the worst thing in the world. One day I'll stop. And one day I'll know exactly whom I'm supposed to like. He'll be standing underneath a perfect tree or something. I mean, the lighting will be exactly right and I'll see what I'm supposed to see. He'll be standing there and I will know. *Know.*

And maybe that will be the same day I stop taking things.

I'll see something and I'll want it. But then I'll think, Oh, Molly, you don't *really* want that. And I'll be in love. Or maybe not love. Maybe just *like*. But I'll at least feel certain about it. And I'll feel fine about everything. One day. Something will happen, and, like magic, my life will be solved.

two

Thursday, October 3

I slam my locker with such force that a freshman standing nearby flinches. It's not that Trigonometry went exceptionally badly; it's that I'm not ready to navigate my lunch conversation with Ruthann Culpepper.

Reluctantly, I thread my way through the throngs of people, keeping an eye out for Henry and Melka. Nowhere. They are nowhere today. Thank God. What would I say? What if Melka exploded in anger and wanted to fight me? Would I fight an exchange student in the hallway over Henry Shaw? No. Well. Maybe.

Before I descend the stairs into the cafeteria I pause on the top step and look out into the segregated landscape. Last year, I didn't care about my popularity, and I'd sit with my friend Sadie Dobyns at any table near the back. We laughed a lot and nothing mattered. Not school dances, or games, or cliques, or clubs. High school was ridiculous; a joke we didn't care about. But this year is different. It all matters.

I'm a Tigerette now. A member of our school's nationally esteemed drill team. Over the summer I practiced my butt off and acquired dance moves, muscle definition, flexibility, and status. I've traded up. Better clothes. Better friends. Better parties. Better crush interests. Grades are slipping, but there's still time to work on that.

I spot Ruthann and Joy. They don't wave. It's not cool to wave. I learned that the first time we ate lunch and they got up to leave and I waved good-bye and Ruthann said, "It's not like we're going off to fight in a war half a world away." And after Ruthann sauntered off, Joy added, in case I had an IQ languishing below seventy, "We never wave."

I join my new friends, placing my lunch sack between them at the table. Ruthann chomps on a salad heavily doused in grated carrots. Joy does the same. I debate whether or not to tell them about making out with Henry. I pull out my turkey sandwich, peel it from its wrapper, and mull over my options. If I tell Ruthann, she'll want every tiny detail. She'll dissect the make-out session until it feels sterile. Then, most likely, she'll judge me. And, inevitably, she'll overstep all boundaries and try to dictate whom I should invite to the Sweetheart Ball. Tate or Henry. She'll want to decide for me. I bet she steers me toward Tate. She's such a steerer. Ugh. Why does our high school even have a girls'-choice dance this early in the year?

Ruthann eyes me knowingly and rakes her fork across her salad, revealing a tomato, which she quickly spears. "I can't believe you didn't call me. You're such a tart."

A tart? Does she know about Henry, or is she randomly calling me a pastry? I take a bite of my sandwich and look confused.

"You're what I call a promiscuous woman," Ruthann says. She smiles at me with her fork still in her mouth. It's frightening.

"Melka told everybody in homeroom," Joy says. "It spread like gangrene."

I hold my head in my hands. "Does this mean I've lost my chance with Tate?" I've been so careful with my Tate crush. Careful to catch his eye when I looked good. Always poised to say funny things when he was in earshot. "My budding romance, is it dead?"

Ruthann laughs. *She laughs.* For the first time since I abandoned my best friend Sadie and climbed up a few rungs on the social ladder, I am deeply missing that forsaken connection. She may have been cynical about school, politics, religion, purebred dogs, and national holidays, but she was always so supportive of me.

"These things happen," Joy says. "That's why I used the gangrene metaphor. Because it's something terrible that just happens too."

"Please, let's not compare my dating situation to gangrene," I say.

"I think Melka was hiding in the garage the whole time," Ruthann says. "I think she's a stalker. You need to start watching yourself."

"Melka won't hurt me," I say. But I'm not totally convinced of that.

"Daughters of diplomats have nothing to lose," Ruthann says. "Watch cable. They off people all the time."

"I don't know about that, but Melka does feel dangerous," Joy says.

Joy nods in affirmation of her own comment, sending her bob bouncing around her face. Great. My closest friend at the moment—short, bouncy, sweet, blond Joy—thinks that Melka should be classified as a dangerous woman.

"I can't believe you swooped in and stole him like that. When did you even start liking Henry? Ever since I've known you you've been obsessed with Tate. *Obsessed*," Joy hisses.

"I know," Ruthann says. "You're such a thief. Who knew?"

My heart begins to race. I don't want to be called a thief. I don't really think my problem is thievery. I didn't *steal* Henry. And I feel bad when I do steal. The urge is unstoppable. Like a thirst. I know that this is weird. And I don't have the words to explain this weirdness to anybody. Joy and Ruthann stare at me. It's time to respond. I shrug. When did lunch turn into a deposition? "Henry is easy to like."

"That's an understatement!" Ruthann says. "Look! They're back together!"

I glance to my left. I can feel my mouth opening in disbelief. Ruthann is right. Henry and Melka exit the cafeteria line together, each holding a plate of fettuccine Alfredo.

"How fickle. You mouth-maul the guy on Wednesday night, and by Thursday he's back with the old girl," Ruthann says. "Carbo-loading! My mother warned me that musicians are like that."

I am stunned. I look at my sandwich and try not to notice when Henry and Melka sit several tables away.

"Are you bummed?" Ruthann asks. Her dark curls fall around her cheeks like she's a well-primped soap opera diva. She's beautiful and intense and she knows it.

"Of course she's bummed," Joy says. She reaches over and pats my leg. "Twelve hours ago she was wrapped in Henry's arms. His mouth on her mouth." Joy puckers her lips in a pained way. "Now they're not even speaking."

"Whoa," I say. "We might still be speaking."

"No," Joy says dramatically. "I don't think you are. This entire situation reeks of tragedy. It's very Greek."

Joy's frenetic energy escapes her body and lands on me, and I now feel terrible. In my mind, the year of making my mark was so much more fun.

I feel a tap on my shoulder and flip around. Tate? Sadie? Tragic Henry? No. A random sophomore girl I don't know.

"Excuse me." She hands us a flyer with a picture of a watch. "I'm Maddie Colfax. This is a watch I lost last week. Have you seen it? I'm offering a reward."

"It's pretty," Joy says. She takes the flyer and studies the photo. "Where did you lose it?"

"Actually, I think somebody took it," Maddie says. "I left it in my locker and it just vanished."

I lean over and squint at the flyer. Fake diamonds. Silver. Head of a snake for the clasp. I didn't take that. A wave of relief washes over me.

"We'll keep an eye out for it," Ruthann says.

Maddie wanders off with her flyers, headed in Tate's direction. I look away as quickly as possible.

"It feels like there's a lot of stuff going missing," Joy says. "Did you see that poster near the office about the lost Chihuahua?"

I didn't take that Chihuahua either.

"Watch thieves, Chihuahua thieves, man thieves," Ruthann says, shooting me a vicious grin. "The world is an imperfect place."

Does she know? She doesn't know. No way. I'm careful. The sound of Henry's laugh pulls my attention to him.

"Let's talk about something else," Ruthann says. She lowers her fork and gets a really intense look on her face. "Next week's game. I am so stressed out about the closing round-off sequence."

Ruthann is regularly stressed out about our round-offs. Only about half of us can do more than four in a row. Yet so far, all of the routines she's designed require six. And as it stands now, the routine for next week's football game only requires twenty-four girls. That means eight of us will be left standing on the sidelines. Tomorrow, Ruthann and Ms. Prufer, our dance coach, will determine who sits out.

"Are you worried about my round-offs?" I ask. I consider them one of my strengths.

"No. I'm thinking about making you the apex point in the final triangle formation," Ruthann says, aiming her fork at me.

During practice, I've never been a point before, let alone

during the apex point final formation. I've always been clumped in the middle. Tucked away with the midperformers. But the apex point is the glory spot. It means I'll be the person who stays on the field the longest. It means I'll be the person who's front and center in the photo that both our school newspaper and the local news-station blog feature after every game. I thought Ruthann might give it to her cousin Deidre, but no. She's going to give it to me.

"I will nail that spot," I say.

Joy isn't told she'll be given even a minor triangle point. To be honest, she does better tucked away in the middle. I have yet to see her complete an entire routine where she doesn't confuse right and left at least one time.

I've barely eaten half my sandwich before Joy stands up.

"I've got to get to Mr. Wonder's class," she says. "I didn't finish setting out the starfish."

I think I detect a tone of hostility in the way Joy says, "starfish." She wasn't supposed to be our science teacher's aide. Ruthann was. But Ruthann's mother called and got things switched so Ruthann could be an office aide instead. After that phone call, Joy was promptly transferred from the attendance office to the biology wing.

"Don't forget to practice your toe-touches tonight," Ruthann says. "Repeatedly."

Joy nods as she walks off.

Ruthann never has to remind me to practice. I'm devoted to my squad. *Devoted.*

"She does the low-clap, high-clap prep all wrong,"

Ruthann says. "And last week she told me that she forgot how to stretch her hip flexors."

Poor Joy. She moves swiftly through the cafeteria and is many tables away. She might not be the most coordinated or flexible or powerful or consistent drill team member, but she's got impeccable posture. You'd never guess she was only five foot three. As she walks up the tiled steps and exits the sunken cafeteria, I'm seized with a weird nostalgic feeling. Even though I'm going to be seeing her again in less than ten minutes, I'm struck by how much I'm going to miss Joy Lowe.

"Don't be late for Wood Shop," I yell, even though she's probably out of earshot. Joy is my shop buddy. We share the table-saw station.

Ruthann rolls her eyes at me. Then she switches gears and her face flushes with excitement. "On a scale of one to ten, how excited are you about your Tate date on Saturday?"

On Saturday, I'll be traveling with Tate to Wyoming, where we're scheduled to ride horses on a scenic trail. It took me a solid three days of asking before my parents agreed to let me go.

"Fourteen. It sounds like a blast," I say. I don't know that much about horses, and I'm actually not that comfortable around big animals, but I figure I should focus on the positive. Tate will be there!

"I wonder what kind of horse you'll be riding. We should ask him right now."

"No," I say. That feels like an unnecessary thing to do in the cafeteria.

"Hey, Tate," Ruthann says. She calls to him twice before he turns around. His blond hair is a gorgeous mess. And he's several tables away, but I can still see his green eyes. It's as if he's lit from the inside. I keep staring. He gives me a quick wave. Even sitting down, Tate has the body of a model. Tall. Athletic. Muscled. It's perfection. Once, while watching a TV show about boxers, Sadie said there are only two types of athletes who can have perfect bodies: basketball players who aren't too tall, and hockey players who still have their teeth. I think she was right.

My attraction delays my reaction time. I give a quick wave back and then glance at the back wall. Because I can't keep lustily staring at Tate. That would be weird. The back wall is plastered with flyers announcing upcoming events. I should take the time to read that wall. Tate laughs, and my gaze follows his voice. Oh, no. I'm staring again. Some basketball players might be too tall, but he isn't. He's amazing-sized. I wonder if he knows he's good-looking. He must.

"Nice hat," Ruthann says.

She's talking to Tate, but he's not wearing a hat. Is this an inside joke? She has a lot of those with guys.

"The hat joke is dying a slow death, Ruthy," he says, giving her a nod. Then he winks at me, which I wasn't expecting, and I quickly glance away again. This time, instead of the back wall, I wind up unintentionally look-ing at Henry and Melka. They are still eating. I hear Tate's laugh again, but I don't turn to look. I feel paralyzed. Like I'm trapped between my two crushes in some sort of doomed crush sandwich. I try to picture happy thoughts. I am in a meadow surrounded by wildflowers.

"Stop acting weird. You and Tate will make a good couple," Ruthann says. "Except he has this one problem that you probably don't know about."

I leave my wildflowers, pull myself out of my meadow, and look at Ruthann. She's staring into a small round mirror and applying lip gloss. She smacks her lips together several times after the second coat.

"What?" I ask. My mind flips through possible deal-breakers. Does he have a girlfriend at a different school? Is he a closet drinker? Could he be addicted to Internet porn? What is Tate's hidden problem?

"He smells," Ruthann says. "Like baloney."

I'm relieved that Tate isn't a closet drinker with a girlfriend and a porn addiction. "I've never noticed a weird odor. And I've smelled him a few times."

Funky body odor could be a deal-breaker. Tate has always been the guy who caught my attention from afar. So if he does smell, I wouldn't know. Whereas Henry is a guy I've been smelling since fourth grade when he used to live on my street. Why am I thinking about Henry again? *Focus on Tate. Focus on Tate.*

Ruthann laughs a little. But it feels like she's laughing at a joke I didn't make.

"Trust me: when we work at the nut house and he has to lean over me to scoop pistachios, his armpits reek. They smell exactly like meat," she says.

Tate's family owns the nut house at the Grand Teton

Mall, where Ruthann works part-time. The thought of Tate leaning over her for any reason, scooping pistachios among them, makes me nauseous.

"Maybe it's his deodorant," I say defensively.

"I don't think Right Guard has a deli meat scent."

Ruthann bites her bottom lip with her two front teeth and slowly shakes her head. "Molly, do you like it when a man smells like meat?"

"Stop messing with me," I say.

"Don't dodge the question," Ruthann says. Her tone is far more serious than it needs to be.

I want to be a triangle point. I don't want to make waves. I go along with her. "I don't smell meat that much. When it comes to the cattle industry, my mom has serious beef reservations. She mainly just cooks free-range chicken."

"God, your mom has serious beef reservations. That's hilarious. You're such a crack-up."

"It's actually the truth," I say.

"Statements like that give me insight into why Tate likes you," Ruthann says.

"My lack of beef consumption?" I ask.

"No. You're quirky. Some guys dig that."

"Thanks," I say.

"Don't thank me. Quirky can be limiting. Some guys detest it."

"Oh," I say. I quickly run down my Crush List to figure out if any of my interests detest quirky. Matt Guthrie? He dressed up like a waffle last year for Halloween. Jamie

Sands? All his still-life paintings in art are of pineapples. Dane Enzo? He wants to be a professional bowler. Curtis Belnap? He wears green shoes. I think I'm safe.

"I've picked a flirt mode with a broader range," Ruthann said.

"Quirky is my flirt mode?" I ask. I didn't realize I had a flirt mode.

Ruthann raises her eyebrows and takes a big sip of milk. "I'm a tease." Two pearls of milk dribble onto her chin.

"And more guys dig that?" I ask.

"Molly, all guys dig that." She dramatically wipes below her mouth with the back of her hand. "That's why strippers make such amazing money."

"Right," I say. But really I'm thinking, Don't female astronauts and brain surgeons and senators make way more than strippers? And don't those careers give you health insurance?

"You're torturing yourself over this Tate and Henry thing, aren't you?"

"No," I lie.

"Go for the one that's available."

I watch Melka and Henry get up to leave.

"Come by the mall tonight. Chat up Tate. You two need to move it to the next level. And I can help."

My eyes grow wide. Helping me and Tate move to the next level seems outside of Ruthann's skill set.

"I can't go to the mall tonight," I say. I stopped going to the mall a few months ago. After I slipped a cheap bracelet into my pocket and got tailed by store security. I put it back before I left. I didn't get approached. But it scared me. It was too close.

"Of course you can come to the mall," she says. She takes a sip of milk. "Listen, for the following demonstration, let's pretend that Henry no longer exists. Okay. You're here." She points to her empty plate. "And Tate's here." She lifts her milk carton high above her head. "That's a lot of distance." She looks down at the plate and then up to the carton. "And I can totally help you bridge it."

"I'm patient," I say. "I think I'll let time do that."

"No," she says. "Isn't this the year that you're making your mark?"

I really regret sharing my ultimate game plan with Ruthann.

"Time matters, Molly. The clock never stops ticking. Bam! You're older than you were two seconds ago. Bam! It happened again. Bam! You'll be a dried-up old woman one day."

I stare at her in disbelief while she yells her final "Bam!"

"Here's my point, Molly." Ruthann sets her milk carton down, laces her fingers together, and looks at me with enough intensity to grill a steak. "Henry is with Melka. You should focus your energy on Tate. But getting to the next level with Tate isn't a guarantee. You might not get there on your own. Come tonight. Seriously. You need me."

I'm a little rattled. I have no idea what Ruthann feels the "next level" with Tate would be, and the prospect of finding out with her assistance scares me. But isn't she right about time passing? Should I just go? And if I don't, isn't Ruthann egotistical enough to take away my triangle point or bench me for the game?

"I'll try," I say.

She smiles. And without further comment, Ruthann Culpepper is up and gone, mingling at a bunch of boy-populated tables. She likes to interact with guys all by herself. I learned this tidbit right away. I also learned that it's my job to dump her tray when she goes rogue like this.

Beep. Beep. Beep. The intercom sounds that lunch is over. Our school doesn't have a bell. We have a synthetic noise, and I'm not really sure what it's supposed to be. Ruthann says it sounds like a robot belching. Again, another on-point Culpepper observation.

I take Ruthann's tray to a row of big gray garbage cans lined with Hefty bags.

"Molly."

I look up and see Henry dumping his tray. I look behind him for Melka, but she's not there.

"Can we talk?" he asks.

That sounds like a simple request. But under these circumstances it's really not. I mean, do I want to talk? If I say yes, does that mean we start talking right now?

We stand there, unintentionally blocking the trash can, forcing people to crowd around the other trash cans in the row. Some kids aim napkins and milk cartons around us. It makes me feel conspicuous. If Melka told everybody in

23

homeroom that I made out with Henry, then I must look like an idiot right now. I turn to leave.

"I can't talk right now," I say. "I've got class."

"Can I walk you?" he asks.

Is he serious? What about Melka? What's wrong with him? He can't have a girlfriend *and* walk me to class. I glance at him and make a confused face, like I'm responding to an offer to fly me to Jupiter or one of her sixty-four moons. Without answering him, I leave.

He races to catch up with me. "Molly, let me walk you to Health Sciences," he says.

I only make it a few steps before I realize that I'm still holding my turkey sandwich. I thought I'd already thrown it away. I feel flustered, but I don't want to turn back around. That would mean I'd have to change course and face Henry and a flood of leaving people. I hurry out of the cafeteria and find a trash can near my locker. I can't believe it. Henry follows me to this trash can too. And to get my attention, he gently touches my arm, and being gently touched by Henry Shaw in this hallway does not release similar sensations from last night's make-out session. No. Gone are the feelings of lust, fire, and fun. Instead, in their place, I'm hit with a muddled mixture of panic, uncertainty, and frustration. *Sexual* frustration? I can't tell.

Before anything can move forward I have to know the answer to one question. So I ask it. "What's up with you and Melka? Are you back together?"

I'm hoping for a quick denial followed by an even quicker explanation. Instead, there's a long pause.

"It's complicated," he says.

Our make-out session flashes through my mind. His face. His room. The floor lamp by my head. *It's complicated?* Wrong answer.

"No," I say, my mind conjuring up an image of Melka. "It's really not." And then I leave Henry Shaw alone in the hallway at a speed that surprises us both.

three

Operation Next-Step-With-Tate has hit a snag. My mother is *not* on board with my plans for Joy to drive me to the mall. In fact, my mother's frown grows so intense that her small chin reveals a colony of concerned dents. She's tucked into her favorite corner of our love seat, holding open a half-finished paperback mystery with her thumb. It's almost six o'clock, and I doubt she's even left the house today. Her hair looks like she hasn't brushed it since yesterday, and the only visible makeup on her face is a crooked smear of coral lipstick.

"I worry about Joy's driving instincts," my mother says. She rubs the dome of her belly and intensifies her frown. "Do you know what I mean?"

"Not really," I lie.

"I ended up driving behind her once to the mall."

"Maybe it wasn't her," I say.

"Of course it was her. She crossed over the center line, and then overcorrected and wandered past the fog line.

And at one point, she nearly forced a bicyclist off the road. Plus, she ran a yellow light."

"What if I drive? I'll buy you a milk shake on the way home."

I know it's going to be hard for my mother to refuse that. As soon as she entered her second trimester, she became an avid fan of the milk shake.

"Be home by nine. And buy two milk shakes. I'll put one in the freezer for tomorrow." She leans back and returns the parted paperback to her nose.

Fabulous. Operation Next-Step-With-Tate is off and running. I brush my hair and put on the tightest clean T-shirt I own. I go light on makeup. I don't like the way foundation, mascara, or eyeliner feels.

I call Joy, and she doesn't object to my offer to drive. Deep down I think she knows that she's lousy behind the wheel. People honk and flip her the bird on a pretty regular basis.

With Tate waiting on the horizon, I feel an urgency to get to the mall. As I grab my purse, my cat, Hopkins, weaves between my legs. I try to take a step forward, but he walks beneath my shoe. Using my other leg, I hop over him and nearly fall.

"I could have broken my neck," I say.

He meows. I think he wants me to play laser mouse with him. When I'm about to leave the house, he often seems to want that.

"I'll play with you when I get back," I say. "I'll be home at nine o'clock."

Hopkins lets out a sigh and crumples to the floor. Once, I read in a magazine article that you should always tell your pets what time you're coming home. It reduces their anxiety. I'm pretty sure it works. Animals are tuned in to something. For instance, elephants are never killed in tsunamis. And a horse can usually predict an electrical storm.

As I attempt to leave, Hopkins tries to slink out the door. I reach down and pet him underneath the chin, gently picking him up by the belly and tossing him several feet away from the threshold.

"Nine o'clock," I repeat. He doesn't like to be touched on the head. It sets off his puma instinct and he becomes all claws.

Pulling into her driveway, I find Joy, thoughtful as usual, waiting for me outside. As I drive us to the mall, she shows me an article that she clipped out of a magazine. "These supplements boost your hair's growth system by sixty percent," she explains. "At that rate, my bob could be to my bra by February."

"What's in February?" I ask.

"Western Drill Team Nationals."

As we exit the car, I think I can actually read Joy's mind. She's picturing herself at nationals with her bra-length hair swept into a fat topknot. She's flipping it back and forth, smiling for the crowd, practically working herself into a state of ecstasy over her ponytail's radiance and girth. I think I hear her moan as we step onto the curb. When she sees me looking at her, her face returns to its usual pleasant and unexcited expression. I think she thinks I think she's weird. But I don't.

My plan at the mall is to avoid entering any store. I'll walk down the center corridor to the nut shop. Chat up Tate. Retrace my steps. And exit the mall without incident. Steering clear of temptation seems like the best strategy.

Joy and I walk through the mall, passing shop after shop. I don't even peek in their windows.

"Ooh!" Joy squeals. "Huge earring sale. Look!"

I don't turn my head. "I'm broke."

Joy doesn't argue, and we keep walking. Mummy and Frankenstein Halloween decorations are taped on the mall's columns. And that creepy fake spiderweb material is draped along the planters and benches. I bet the stores are decked out too. I'll never know.

"There's a closeout on all sandals," Joy says, pointing to another store. "Don't you want to take a quick stroll through the inventory?"

"It's October and we live in Idaho. Not interested," I say.

"God," Joy says. "You're so focused."

Was that a compliment? It doesn't matter. I can see the nut house in the distance. And as soon as I spot Tate, my crush feelings return. Forget Henry Shaw. I'll pretend that I never made out with him. I'll trick my heart by placing it in a time machine and maneuvering around the make-out session entirely. I'm in control of which guy I like. And I plan to resettle on my interest on gorgeous, athletic, well-traveled Tate.

29

"What's wrong?" Joy asks. "Why are you slowing down?"

I stop walking. "I'm excited," I say.

"Yeah," Joy says. "Tate's a stud."

"And he just keeps getting studlier. I mean, he's wearing an apron and hairnet and he still looks hot."

I fluff my hair and pull my T-shirt down a little, positioning the V-neck closer to the top of my cleavage.

"Speaking of hot, look who's in the food court."

I look, half expecting to see Henry. Which is weird, because I know Joy doesn't find him hot.

"Roy Ekles," Joy says. "At that table by the front doors. What's he doing?"

I see Roy leaning back in a chair. He's putting something that resembles french fries into his mouth. "Eating?" I say. Roy is what I'd consider part of the alternative crowd. Until two months ago he had blue hair and wore clothes with an absurd number of zippers. He still wears weird clothes, but with his hair dyed a conservative brown color, at least his head appears more mainstream. Perhaps it's just a phase. Does Joy want to date somebody with blue hair?

"What do you think of him?" Joy leans into me when she asks me this, so much so that I can smell her bubblegum breath.

"He looks better now that he looks normal."

Joy leans further into me, so I'm supporting most of her weight. "He looks fantastic."

She sounds really into him. Which surprises me, because I didn't know she was into anybody. Since we've become friends she hasn't mentioned any guys.

"Are you thinking about asking him to the Sweetheart Ball?" I ask.

She sounds caught off guard by my question and stands up straight. "We're not *there* yet."

If she's not "there" with Roy, I wonder where exactly she is with him.

We leave him in the food court and keep walking to our destination. We're so close to the nut house now that both Ruthann and Tate spot us. Suddenly I feel underprepared. "I don't even know what we should talk about."

"Don't show up with an agenda. Just buy a bunch of nuts and see what happens." Joy squeezes my arm reassuringly. "See you in fifteen."

"Aren't you coming with me?" I ask. Why am I tracking him down the Thursday before our date? I'm awkward. I should try to have as little contact as possible with him until we make it to our horses in Wyoming.

"Yeah, I'll catch up with you," she says. "It's not like the nut shop is going anywhere. I want to get my vitamins."

She doesn't wait for any kind of permission to abandon me. She just does it. So I walk solo up to the nut shop.

"Look who's here," Ruthann says.

She wipes down the white Formica countertop, while Tate places newly dipped caramel apples on a glass display shelf. Nestled atop small squares of waxed paper, they look delicious.

"Are you here to talk to Tate?" she asks me.

My ear tips burn. Is this an ambush? Because that question does nothing to make me interact with Tate more effectively or move us to the next level. It makes me feel like a moron.

"I came for nuts," I say.

Ruthann looks amused.

"What kind?" she asks. "Hazelnuts, Brazil nuts, macadamia nuts, cashews, pistachios—"

When she pauses for a breath, I interrupt. "I need a minute," I say.

"Take a minute," she says, then looks at the wall clock behind her.

While I survey the nuts, Ruthann rubs the cloth so hard against the countertop that it squeaks.

"Where's Joy?" Tate asks. "I thought I saw her with you."

"I think she's at the GNC," I say.

"What for? The only people I ever see in there are middle-aged couples and sometimes a rogue elderly person," Ruthann says.

Ruthann should not be jumping into my conversation with Tate. This entire situation feels lame.

"She wants hair vitamins," I explain.

"Like prenatal vitamins?" Ruthann says. "Hey, Tate, did you know Molly's mom is pregnant? She's forty-four. Isn't that wild? It was an oops."

I'm stunned. Ruthann's idea of taking things with Tate to the next level apparently involves disclosing personal information about my parents' baby-making habits. I can feel myself blushing. It's not that I'm exactly embarrassed that my mother is going to have a baby, it's just that I didn't venture out to the nut shop to discuss her gestation cycle with Tate.

"Hey, Ruthy," Tate says, handing her a large metal bowl coated in congealed caramel. "Why don't you take this in the back and scrub it down?"

"Oh, I'll do that when we close," Ruthann says, reaching into the roasted almond bin and popping one in her mouth.

"Why wait?" he asks. "I'll keep an eye on the front."

She takes the messy bowl in one hand and huffs into the back room.

"Which nuts were you interested in?" he asks.

I look at mound after mound of warm, tumbling nuts.

"Maybe pecans," I say, tapping my finger on the glass in front of a long heaping row of them.

"Our pecans are good, but have you ever tried our cinnamon peanuts? We roasted them this afternoon, right in the back."

"Wow, you roast your own nuts."

"No, that would be painful. We just roast these," he says, burying the curved tip of a metal scoop deep into a peanut pile.

The burning sensation in my ear tips increases. When I crush on a guy I become such a dweeb.

"You know what I meant," I say. "I'll take a quarter pound of your pistachios."

He scoops up a small mound of nuts and pours them into a white paper bag. He doesn't weigh them. He just eyeballs it.

"On the house," he says. As he hands me the bag, I watch

his arms. His skin is so much tanner than mine. He went to Morocco over the summer for a month. That's what I'm looking at. His sexy Moroccan tan.

"I don't mind paying," I say.

"I'll keep that in mind on our date."

Again, my ears are so hot they feel like they could fall off. I can't believe I have this much blood in my entire body, let alone in my head region.

"Hey, Tate," Joy says.

I look up. Saved by Joy.

"Wow," Ruthann says, emerging from the back room. "You really did come to the mall."

"Yeah," Joy says. "I needed some mall stuff."

"So, did you practice before you came? Are you going to practice after? Or maybe you're going to practice right now? In front of the nut house?" Ruthann says.

Joy looks embarrassed. I try to smooth things over. "We'll get some practice in tonight." I look at Tate and try to communicate that everything is cool, that girls in drill team sometimes call each other out. It's how we bond.

Ruthann tilts her head with a fierce amount of incredulity. "Listen, Joy. Your round-offs suck. And you've got some sort of compass disorder where you're incapable of either identifying or facing north. And you don't even seem to notice. Or care."

This feels so harsh. And awkward. And ongoing.

"I care," Joy says. "I practice all the time."

That's not really true, but I don't want to say anything to escalate the dustup.

"It's getting late," I say. "Maybe we should head home." I am not accomplishing anything at the mall.

"And can we not talk to customers like that?" Tate adds.

"They aren't customers," Ruthann says.

"Actually," Joy says, "I might buy some nuts."

"Whatever," Ruthann says.

"I'll give you some of mine," I say. "Let's go." I turn and look at Joy. "Let's not antagonize the situation." Which I regret saying after I say it, because I think it means I'm siding with Ruthann. But really I'm siding with myself. I'm ready to leave.

"Oh, Tate, you should let your mother know that we're low on straws," Ruthann says.

Tate doesn't look at her. "I'll let her know."

She picks up the rag and starts re-wiping the counters.

"See you guys later," I say. Even though Ruthann finds it annoying, I decide to wave. Tate waves back and smiles. He looks so cute when he waves. I'm relieved that the girl drama doesn't seem to have driven him off.

Joy strides through the mall's long central hallway without saying a single word. It's like her anger toward Ruthann has spread to me. But that's not fair. I can't control Ruthann's outbursts. Sometimes she's just mean. And it's illogical for Joy to hold that against me. As we turn the corner and approach the exit, Joy's shoulder snags one of those creepy, artificial spiderwebs, tearing ten feet of it from the wall. I watch the tiny threads blow in the breeze behind her while we walk to the car.

"You've got a cobweb on you," I say.

She doesn't respond or seem to care.

Even when I'm driving, there's complete silence. A mile ticks by.

"You'll have to let me know if those vitamins work," I say.

"I don't feel like talking about my hair," Joy says.

"Well—"

Joy cuts me off. "I don't feel like talking at all."

I've only driven to her house a few times. As I turn down elm-lined streets, sorting my way through the suburbs, she doesn't help guide me. I just guess through all the turns. When I finally pull into her driveway, she remains quiet. As I turn to say good-bye, I notice that she's crying.

"Don't cry," I say. "What happened tonight isn't that big a deal." I try to say what I'd want to hear under similar conditions.

"You don't get it," Joy says.

"Oh, I get it," I say. "Ruthann can be volatile."

Joy laughs like I've said something stupid. "I thought you were going to be a different kind of friend."

"What do you mean?" I ask. We've only been friends for a little while, and I've been a great friend to her. Sort of.

"I thought you were going to be real," Joy says. She gets out of my car and shuts the door so lightly that I'm not sure it's totally closed.

I lower my window.

"I *am* real," I say. Only after the words leave my mouth do I feel a little lame.

Joy turns around. Maybe I got through to her. "No. All you care about is being a stupid apex triangle point."

I gasp. That is *not* all I care about, though I do think it's pretty cool. I shift the car into park and open up my door.

"You're totally wrong," I say.

Joy looks at me like she couldn't care less. How did this situation, a simple trip to the nut shop, escalate to the point where my closest friend is sobbing on her front lawn and spitting insults at me? I'm never going to the mall again.

"I'm not wrong. And I'm not dumb either."

"I never said you were dumb."

"But you think I am," she says emphatically.

I do think this. But I don't admit it. "I don't think you're dumb at all." For some reason I close my eyes while I'm talking.

"You're lying. That's why you closed your eyes!"

I open my eyes. "No."

"I am so done with this. Ruthann. Tigerettes. You. I'm over it!"

Me? How did things get here? How can she be over me? "Wait." But she doesn't wait.

I watch Joy slip behind an ornate white door, her wispy blond hair trailing behind her. Then she's gone, swallowed by her house. I stare at that door, hoping it might swing back open, allowing for a more levelheaded Joy to emerge. But no. She's not coming out.

As I drive home, I feel sad and defeated. Tears burn behind

my eyes, and I try hard to push everything to a place deep inside of me, beneath my skin, beneath my bones. High school shouldn't be this hard. Last year sucked because it was boring. Sadie and I sat around as certified outsiders, ridiculing everyone. And now this year sucks even worse. My life feels impossible, and it's only October.

I walk through the front door and both of my parents are seated on the couch. They look up at me as I stride to my bedroom, refusing to make small talk.

"No milk shake?" my mom asks.

"No," I say. "The mall sucked so bad that I forgot."

"She's dating," my mother explains to my father.

I stop walking and turn around. "I'm not dating."

"Does this mean your horseback trip got canceled?" my father asks.

I turn around. "No." Why would my father say such a thing? I would be devastated if my date with Tate was canceled.

"Don't you want some dinner?" asks my mom.

I don't feel like eating. I don't feel like talking. I just feel rotten. "Maybe later."

I walk into my room and open my jewelry box. I take out a pearl ring and slip it on. I crawl into bed and turn it over and over around my finger. This was Sadie's ring. She has no idea that I took it. It's one of the few things I really regret taking. But it happened. I snagged it one day and never knew how to give it back. And it feels wrong to let it rest hidden in a drawer. A ring should be worn. Even if it's just to bed. I turn it over again, thinking of Sadie. And

Joy. It's been a long time since I've felt this defeated. But the year of making my mark is still repairable. Life is long. I can fix my friendship with Joy. And probably Sadie too. Deep down, they know I'm a good friend. I just need to show them.

four

I am not a triangle point. I'm clumped in the middle, struggling through practice. In the gymnasium the air feels swampy. And even though it's a brisk temperature outside, inside on the basketball court, where we're going over and over and over our routine, it feels ridiculously hot. Like summer in Florida. Or the Gobi desert. Normally when things get challenging, I have an ally. But Joy didn't even come today. I wonder if she'll quit the Tigerettes. She seemed genuinely hurt. Should she? Should *I?* Ruthann puffs on a whistle, signaling that it's time to form our first position. She puffs on the whistle a second time—urgently—because she thinks we aren't moving fast enough. Oh my god. I think my life would feel better if I quit.

"Let's practice without traveling!" Ruthann barks.

During the learning phase of the routine, I'm always surprised that some girls have a tough time traveling from their first assigned spots to their second assigned spots, and so on, while executing the arm sequences at the same time.

"Five, six, seven, eight!" Ruthann calls.

We unleash our arm moves. Straight out. Straight up. Drop to our sides. Triple clap. Repeat. Double clap. Punch at the crowd. Jab. Jab. Jab.

"I see sloppy arms! Hit those points! Be fierce!"

We slap and clap and jab over and over.

"Now do it while traveling! Make the circle. And rotate!"

Ruthann paces in front of us while Ms. Prufer sits in the stands. How do they choose who's good enough? I am rotating within my circle position and punching the crap out of my jabs. It's time for the kick sequence. I kick with such intensity that my stomach muscles cramp. I will not be cut from my first game. I will not.

"Deidre! Where are you going?" Ruthann calls. "You're making the circle look like a cancer cell. Way too much irregular growth. Come back!"

I can't believe in our final position that Deidre is a triangle point.

"All right! Let's take a break!"

Ruthann flips around and bounces over to sit next to Ms. Prufer. They're talking about us. Judging us and our traveling abilities and our kicks and arms. We haven't even done any tumbling yet. I walk to the sidelines and grab my water. The room is definitely way too hot. I can feel sweat dripping down my back. This is how I spend fourth period now every other day. I don't take a regular gym class. I attend Tigerette practice and receive credit for PE. Our school alternates between A day and B day, four classes each day, eight classes total. It's tough to keep everything straight. Basically, the system sucks.

"Molly!" Ruthann yells. "Can you come here?"

She is in a terrible mood. I was so afraid of talking to her at lunch that I bought a banana and went to the library to eat it, even though food isn't permitted in there.

"Yeah?" I trot across the courts, in her direction.

"Missed you at lunch," she says, standing up.

"I was studying," I say, "in the library."

Ruthann rolls her eyeballs impatiently. "Don't lie to me. I saw you in there trying to eat a banana surreptitiously."

"I just needed a break," I say. "Life feels crazy right now." In order to avoid making eye contact, I play with the hem of my shorts. Her gaze is so powerful.

"Crazy?" Ruthann says, and takes one intimidating step closer to me. "So I take it you've heard the bad news?"

At the word *news*, I look up. Ruthann squints, making her brown eyes appear slanted and venomous. If I were a prairie dog or small rodent, I'd be dead by now.

"Is it about Joy?" I ask. I'm suddenly worried that something "crazy" has happened to her. That must be why she is absent.

"Sort of," Ruthann says.

I cover my mouth and gasp.

"I know," Ruthann says. "It's terrible. You and Joy got me fired from the nut shop." She slowly shakes her head in disbelief. Then she reaches out and grabs my arm. "I've lost my job."

"Really?" I say, trying to sound surprised, but I'm not that surprised. Ruthann was a total bitch last night.

"Joy won't even take my calls. And she's skipped today.

Can you believe that? Just like you said: it's crazy."

Ruthann is still clamped on to me above the elbow, and I try to shake her grip loose by shrugging several times and lightly swinging my arm.

"Has she talked to you?" she asks.

"No, I think she's pretty upset about how things went down last night."

Ruthann lets go of my arm and waves her hand around like she's preparing to fence with me without using a sword.

"Her round-offs suck. And so do her toe touches. It's my job to tell her that."

I take another drink of water and look out at the basketball court. Some of the girls are gathering at our starting positions.

"But I think you hurt her feelings," I say. Even in Joy's absence, I want to prove to her that I'm not a fake person.

"Am I just supposed to stand back and let her suck? Great strategy, Molly. I bet the judges will love to see one member sucking so badly. Maybe we could get a trophy for that. Do they give a trophy for almost-first-place-except-you-had-a-member-who-sucked?"

Ruthann needs to get a life. Or keep this life and begin seeking out a career in improving people's flexibility by making them feel like utter crap.

"Why are you looking at me like that?" Ruthann asks.

I shrug. "I should probably take my spot." I watch as Deidre trips and almost falls. And then I hear myself asking a question that I thought I was only thinking. "You're going to give me Deidre's triangle point, right? You're just waiting until the last minute? Making me sweat it out?"

Ruthann snorts. "Is that all you care about? What about the fact that I'm losing a paycheck every week now?"

"I care," I say. "But there's really nothing I can do."

"Of course there is," Ruthann says. "Either you or Joy need to talk to Tate and tell him it was a big misunderstanding. Preferably, both of you should. Okay?"

"Can we discuss this later?" I ask.

"Absolutely," Ruthann says. "I'll drive you home after school."

I return to my spot, walking across the cushioned gymnastics mats. My stomach feels knotted.

"Are you sick?" Deidre asks me.

I shake my head. And the world moves double-time.

"You look pale," Deidre says.

"I don't tan well," I say.

"I'm not joking," Deidre says. "I think you need fresh air."

"Yeah," I say. "The room is so hot."

"It's regular temperature," Deidre says. "I think there's something wrong with you."

"No," I say.

I am now looking at two Deidres. And I feel like I might throw up. I don't want to vomit on the court. Then I'll be the day's gossip. I run into the hallway and slam open the bathroom door. I barely make it to the trash can before I hurl up my banana. I always sort of knew that one day Ruthann Culpepper would make me puke.

While my head is still inserted in the trash can, a toilet

flushes and Sadie exits one of the stalls. She glances at me. I haven't seen Sadie, I mean, really seen her, in weeks. Her hair is down, and she's wearing a plain gray T-shirt. No jewelry. Sadie hardly ever wears jewelry. When it comes to fashion, she's just so mellow.

"Are you okay?" she asks.

I don't really know what to say. I know she's only talking to me because she feels like she's supposed to, not because she actually wants to have a conversation with me.

"I'm puking," I say.

"I can see that," Sadie says. "Do you need any help?"

I wipe my mouth with the back of my hand.

"It's basically a one-woman job," I say.

"I'm trying to be nice to you," Sadie says. "Is dance team practice too intense?"

I'm not on the dance team. I'm on the drill team. And she's aware of that. Our dance team carries weird streamers, wears unitards, and are mocked relentlessly. I know, because Sadie and I used to mock them.

"I'm actually on the drill team and practice is going awesome," I say. Because I can't admit to her how much it actually sucks.

"Looks like it," Sadie says.

I lift my head up and really stare at her. And I realize something. That person I used to be. And that person she used to be. They just don't exist anymore. It's just like we learned in Sociology last semester. People are evolving all the time. And Sadie Dobyns and Molly Weller have evolved into completely different people.

"You're so rude," I say.

"I was actually trying to be nice," she counters.

"I didn't realize being a decent person required focused effort," I say.

"Why are you acting like this?"

"I'm sick," I say. I hurl again. Sadie calmly shuts the water off. I lift my head out of the can in time to see her flick her wet fingers in the sink and pull a paper towel out of the wall unit.

She doesn't say anything else. She wads the towel and sets it in the trash can on top of my puke. She walks out of the bathroom and leaves me alone. The hinges release a sad-sounding creak as the door sweeps closed behind her.

I breathe deeply several times and then splash some cold water on my face. As I lean against the white tiled walls and focus on breathing, I see an earring. It sits on the sink ledge in an indentation intended to restrain a bar of soap. I reach out and finger the cold metal, poking my thumb against the blunt end of the earring's post. *Do I want this?* The door swings open and I pull my hand back. It's Mrs. Pegner, the school nurse.

"Are you okay?" she asks. "We had a report that some-body was sick in here."

"It's me," I say. "I'm the one who's sick in here."

She nods her gray head and walks to me.

"Let's get you to the office and call your mom."

"Okay," I say. "Wait. Somebody left this."

I pick up the gold earring and it dangles from my fingers like a tiny chandelier.

"It's a nice one," she says. "I'll drop it at the Lost and Found."

Mrs. Pegner takes it from me and slips it into her pocket. An intense calm sweeps over me. It's a more intense calm than when I realized I hadn't stolen that sophomore's missing watch. I'm elated. Because I wanted that earring and I didn't take it. Right now it's on a journey to a box, where its rightful owner may eventually track it down. Maybe this is my turning point. Mrs. Pegner hooks her arm around my waist and leads me out of the bathroom, around the corner, and down the long, orange, carpeted hallway to the nurse's office.

It smells like spearmint mouthwash in here. I wonder why? I swallow. Actually, my mouth feels like it could use some spearmint mouthwash. I look around the room for a bottle of Listerine. The only bottles in here are two plastic two-liter containers of Pibb Zero.

As I lie on the cot, waiting for my recently phoned mother, I see Tate Arnold. He walks into the room and approaches my cot. With his shirt only half tucked, he looks amazing. And also surprised to see me.

"What's wrong?" he asks. "Did you hurt yourself in practice?"

He crouches down a little. But not enough. I'm basically looking at his knees.

"No. Things got a little overheated in the gym," I say. I'm worried that he's going to think I'm too sick to go on our date tomorrow. Lying down on a cot during fourth period must make me look ridiculously ill.

"Can I get you anything?" he asks.

"No."

"I can't hang around and talk. Party in Calculus. We all passed our exam on inverse trigonometric functions. They sent me to collect the Pibb."

I nod. "You'll need ice," I say, pointing to the counter. I wish I was at a party. I don't go to enough parties. My school social calendar relies too much on Ruthann and drill team. I need to figure out ways to beef it up. Maybe I should volunteer somewhere and meet a bunch of new people. Do I have time to volunteer somewhere? Would I enjoy spending a few hours a week in a hospital?

Tate picks up the Pibb Zero bottles and acts like he's going to juggle them for me, but he doesn't.

"You're still picking me up at ten tomorrow morning, right?" I ask.

"Are you going to be up for horseback riding?" he asks.

"Absolutely," I say.

"Okay," Tate says. "And there's one other thing I forgot to mention."

I hate it when people forget to mention things.

"My brother and his girlfriend want to come. Is that cool?"

I've seen Tate's older brother, Wyatt, and his girlfriend, Denise, on multiple occasions at a juice bar near school. They're the closest thing Idaho has to hippies, and I bet I'll like them both fine. I don't care if they come.

"Sure," I say.

"Hey," Tate says, lightly tapping the side of my cot with

48

his leg, "I'll call you later." He carries the soda bottles into the hallway and disappears. He looks even more tan than last night. How is that possible? Does he spray-tan?

I close my eyes. I need to figure out a phenomenal way to ask Tate to the dance. Balloons? No. Not phenomenal. Way too many people use balloons. A funny card? No. Something bigger. A stuffed animal? No. Those aren't sexy. What's a sexy and phenomenal way to ask a guy to a dance? My thoughts are violently interrupted by the sensation of somebody plopping down next to me on the cot.

"I saw him come in here," Ruthann says. "What did you tell him?"

I blink at her. "I told him where he could find the Pibb."

"And then? What about my job?" she asks.

"It didn't come up," I say.

"You can't be that sick," Ruthann says.

"Actually, I think I am," I say.

The sound of somebody knocking makes Ruthann stop talking and turn around.

"We need to let our patient rest," Mrs. Pegner says.

"Yes. I really need rest," I say.

Ruthann reluctantly gets up. "I'm going to call you later."

"I hope I'm feeling well enough to talk," I say.

Ruthann frowns at that. As I rest my head back down, there's a soft knock at the door.

"You are a very popular sick person," Mrs. Pegner says.

"It's probably somebody looking for more Pibb," I explain.

"Molly?"

The voice is so distinct that my skin erupts in goose pimples.

"Henry?" I prop myself up on my elbows. "What are you doing here?"

He walks into the office and stands next to me. My heart begins to race. That whole pep talk I gave myself yesterday at the mall that I was completely over Henry and didn't care about him and that my heart had entered a time machine and was now unaffected by our make-out session—all that was a lie. I am so attracted to Henry right now. Even though he's wearing geeky clothes and looks, well, a little geeky.

"I was headed to the attendance office and I saw you through the door," he says. "Are you okay?"

I ignore his question and ask my own. "Why were you headed to the attendance office?" Because that's where people go to get permission slips for absences. Is he planning on being absent?

He shifts his weight. He looks uncomfortable. "I had to get slips. For Monday."

He said the word *slips*. That's the plural form of *slip*. Why would he need more than one slip? Is he going away on a long trip? With somebody? My mind leaps to Melka.

"Are you and Melka going somewhere?" I ask. It hurts to even form that question, because I want the answer to be no. And if the answer isn't no, I'm going to feel a little crushed.

He pauses. His eyes look at five or six things in the room. Lamp. Floor. Desk. Light switch. Shoes. Me.

"It's complicated," Henry says.

My elbows ache from supporting my body weight, so I lie back down on the crunchy pillow. I am so sick of hearing about how complicated things are between Melka and Henry. And why does he keep tracking me down to tell me about how complicated they are? The cafeteria garbage can. My sick cot. I wasn't seeking out a Henry/Melka status check.

"What are you doing in here, Henry? This girl is sick and needs to be left alone. She vomited in the girls' bathroom," Mrs. Pegner says.

I'm really surprised to hear her divulge this information to Henry, because I thought your medical history, even if it was something that happened five minutes ago in a public bathroom, was strictly confidential.

"Can I call you later?" Henry asks.

I want to say yes. I want to say yes. "I'm sick," I say.

"Out," Ms. Pegner says. "With all these interruptions she'll never recover."

I watch Henry leave, and the pocket of excitement he brought with him drifts out the door as he goes. Melka and Henry. Melka and Henry. How can I still be falling for him?

"Molly?" my mother calls. She's standing in the doorframe, wearing lavender maternity clothes that barely seem to fit. She looks like a blooming lilac bush. "Is it the stomach flu?"

I shake my head.

"I didn't sleep well last night," I lie. "I think I'm worn down."

"Do you want anything to eat?"

"I just want my bed."

I rise from the cot and walk to her. And when she hugs me I almost cry. The feeling comes out of nowhere. But I'm overcome with gratitude. There are a variety of mothers in the world, and I was lucky enough to end up with a dedicated one. She dropped everything to come and get me. "Thanks," I whisper into her neck. I can feel her stomach pressing against me.

"We can't go straight home. We need to stop by the store first. I need to deliver the payroll to your dad."

five

When my father first bought the Thirsty Truck eight years ago, I thought, Cool. I can eat all the candy I want and not have to pay for it. But that's not how things worked out. Running a convenience store is a terrible way to make a living, unless you like being married to a cash-strapped corner shop that overcharges people for bleach, toilet paper, and Ritz crackers. I basically never see my dad, and when I do he's stressed out. Complaining about profit margins. Slacker employees. And the forever malfunctioning shaved-ice machine. My mother does most of his paperwork and calls herself his bookkeeper. In short, the stress is a family affair and it never ends.

As my mother pulls into a parking spot, instead of entering the Thirsty Truck, I decide I'd rather wait in the car.

"Don't you want something to settle your stomach?" she asks as she gathers the folder from under her seat.

"Just air." I reach beneath my seat for the reclining lever and I lower myself into a position where I can sleep.

"Molly, if you're too sick to enter the store, your father

53

is not going to let you go horseback riding tomorrow."

I relocate the reclining lever and bring myself to an upright position. She's right. My dad has been looking for an excuse to kill the horseback riding trip ever since he agreed to let me go. I still remember his response when I told him that that trip would take place in Wyoming.

"Can't you date within state lines? Why do you want to ride a horse? And shouldn't Tate ask *me* for *my* permission?"

It's as if my father had fallen out of a television sitcom. "*Your* permission? That's weird. It's not like we're getting married."

"I've talked to his mother," my mom offered.

"What does Molly know about horses?" my father asked.

I thought I'd caught him at a good time. He'd looked relaxed, watching a crime drama with my mom. She'd already said it sounded like a fun opportunity. Of course, she said we needed my dad's permission. Of course, as soon as I asked him for it, the scene on the television exploded in gunfire. White pops of light burst from the muzzles of long guns. A botched bank robbery. Half the people fell down dead. I moved to block my parents' view and sat cross-legged in front of them.

"I've been on other dates," I said. "I'm almost seventeen."

"Wyoming?" my father asked.

We lived very near the Wyoming/Idaho border. It wasn't much more than an hour's drive. My father was completely overreacting, and my mother knew it.

"Sounds like a great time," she said. "And they're going

as part of a group. It's not like she'll be off on her own in the middle of the wilderness."

My father didn't want to agree. But he didn't have reasonable grounds left to object.

"Take your cell phone and keep it on," he said.

"You bet," I said, though I suspected my mountain date with Tate would be taking me out of range.

The glass doors chime when we walk inside the store. Behind the register, I spot my father, decked out in a red smock, selling a ton of sprinkle doughnuts. We smile at each other. For some reason, our town has gone wild for sprinkle doughnuts. They regularly sell out. The sprinkle colors appear irrelevant to their popularity. I suspect it's their high-sugar content. Whatever it is, our town has become addicted.

I wander to the ice cream section. Doesn't that settle stomachs? As I survey the different pints, one particular flavor catches my eye. Red velvet cake. It's a limited-edition flavor. Oh, that stuff is criminally good. I can't ever say no to it. Which is when one of the best ideas I've had in a long time hits me. This is how I should invite Tate to the Sweetheart Ball. I'll write a note that says, "You'll have to eat it all if you want to go to the Sweetheart Ball with . . ." And then I'll write a second note and wrap it up in plastic, and it will say, "Molly Weller!" I'll put that at the bottom of the pint. What a cleverly delicious idea. I pull two pints out of the freezer. Because I love the flavor too much to give my only pint away.

"Sadie!" my mother says behind me. "It's been too long."

I flip around. Why is she here? Why isn't she in school? It doesn't get out for another half hour. I watch my mother hug her. Even though I should approach them, I don't. But then I see them point at me, and I hate the idea of them talking about me behind my back. So I join them.

"Thanks for calling me about Molly," my mother says.

I blink. "You've been calling my mother?"

"This afternoon," my mother says. "When you were sick."

"Oh," I say. I thought Mrs. Pegner called my mom. I thought Sadie had dried her hands, gone to class, and washed her conscience of me.

"Molly," Sadie says. Her voice is loud and serious, the tone of voice she assumes when she's about to make an announcement. Is she going to say something loud and serious right in front of my mother? This is so weird.

"I'm glad we ran into each other. I've been meaning to track you down for a while. I think you've got something of mine," Sadie says.

I am stunned that she would do this to me in my family's store. Her words echo in my head. "You've got something of mine." It feels like my life is ending. Really? This is how you're going to confront me? At my father's convenience store? Really? I am mad and confused at the same time. Because why did I even steal her ring? Nothing makes sense. So I do what I always planned to do if I were ever caught. I deny everything. Passionately.

"I have no idea what you're talking about," I say. "I don't have anything of yours. I'm certain. I live a scarce

56

existence. The only things I have in my life are the things I absolutely need."

"Like two pints of red velvet ice cream," Sadie says jokingly.

It's interesting that she would joke with me at the same time she is trying to ruin my life.

"I'm asking Henry to the Sweetheart Ball using the ice cream," I say. Maybe I can distract her from busting me as a thief in front of my mother by tossing out other interesting news.

"You're asking Henry Shaw to the Sweetheart Ball?" Sadie asks. "Isn't he dating that exchange student?"

Both my mother and Sadie are looking at me. I stop breathing. Did I say Henry? I didn't say Henry.

"You're asking your study partner to the dance?" my mother asked. "Our old neighbor?"

No. No. No. This tongue slip doesn't require any elaboration or comment.

"I meant Tate," I said. "I'm asking Tate."

My mother and Sadie are still focused on me. I hate it. I didn't mean to say Henry. I didn't.

"Are you going to the dance?" my mom asks Sadie.

I can't help myself from releasing an obnoxious-sounding snort. That's ninety percent of the reason I'm no longer friends with Sadie, I think. She doesn't give a rip about important high school milestones.

"Yeah, I'm going with a friend. Ansel," Sadie says.

Who the heck is Ansel, and when did Sadie start going to high school events? I'm blown away.

"Who's Ansel?" my mother asks.

"I met him this summer. When I was staying with my grandparents. We both volunteered at Craters of the Moon."

I had no idea Sadie was volunteering at Craters of the Moon. That's nuts. That place is for tourists who want to stand on a lava field and take photos that make it look like they're walking on top of the lunar surface. I can't believe Sadie spent ten minutes there, let alone a summer.

"I've always enjoyed Craters of the Moon," my mother says.

This is too much. Why is my mother sucking up to Sadie Dobyns? On the bright side, this conversation does keep Sadie from ratting me out.

"It was life-changing," Sadie says.

I can't listen to another word of this. "My ice cream is melting." I turn to go to the register.

Sadie reaches out and touches me, and an electric shock shoots through me. "Hold on. Back to that item that I left at your house."

No. Not here. Not now. Can't we talk about this in private? Isn't that where people admit things of this nature? I imagine the conversation going this way. We're alone in a dark room. The confession comes quickly and bluntly.

Sadie: I know you stole my ring.
Me: You're right.
Sadie: Why did you do it?
Me: I don't know. I think I might be a kleptomaniac.
Sadie: That's terrible.

Me: I feel anxious all the time.
Sadie: Is there anything I can do?
Me: Can you forgive me?
Sadie: Yes. Completely.

I can tell by the tone in Sadie's voice that we are not going to have that perfect and magical conversation that concludes with forgiveness at the Thirsty Truck.

"I left a pair of my shoes at your house. My red sandals."

"I saw those the other day in your room," my mother says.

"Oh," I say, relieved and surprised and defensive. "I don't know how they got there." I need to relax. Breathe. Breathe. "Do you want me to bring them to school for you? Maybe Monday? Now that it's fall, they're probably not in heavy rotation."

My mind flashes to all of the things, besides the ring, that I've taken from Sadie's house: a hummingbird figurine, a refrigerator magnet from Niagara Falls, one of her mother's knitting needles. I wish I could explain that I didn't set out to take any of these things. Stealing isn't something I choose to do.

"Sure. Monday," Sadie says. "I better get going. Ansel is in the car."

"Wow. You cut last class to be with a guy?" I ask.

Behaviorally speaking, I don't even recognize Sadie. She must be going through some sort of gushing hormone spurt.

"There was a bomb threat," Sadie says. "Everyone was asked to leave. Except some of the kids who were dropped off are still waiting in the football stadium for their parents."

"That's the third bomb threat this year," I say. "I wonder who's phoning them in?"

Sadie shrugs. "Probably just some random idiot."

My mother and Sadie give each other a warm hug. Sadie takes two sodas to the counter and doesn't say good-bye to me.

"Why is Ansel waiting in the car?" I ask. If I was dating a guy I'd expect him to enter stores with me. Especially if I was buying him a soda.

"He sprained his ankle rock climbing. He's not very mobile," Sadie says.

What on earth has happened to Sadie? She's dating a rock climber? Does she climb rocks? I take a quick look at her fingernails to see if they look beat up. No. They look regular.

"I hope he feels better soon," my mom says.

"Thanks," Sadie says.

As we watch Sadie leave, my mother looks almost despondent. She's going to ask me about the Sadie rift again. I haven't been able to give her a satisfying answer yet as to why I terminated our friendship. My mother doesn't understand my newly realized high school ambitions. She thinks of high school as prep time for college. But high school matters. I want to make something of myself here. Before she can probe me with Sadie questions, I take the conversation in a different direction.

"Maybe you should let me drive to school. During bomb

threats, I'd be able to drive myself and other innocent students to safety."

"Sitting in the bleachers isn't the end of the world, Molly."

Just then, a lightning bolt cracks open the sky and rain begins pouring down in dense, hard-hitting sheets.

"It is if you get struck by lightning," I say.

She sighs. She can't argue with that.

"I'm going to grab some ice cream too," my mother says. "Do you want me to snag you an additional pint?"

"I'm set with two," I say. While pregnant, my mother has become an amazingly reckless eater of frozen dairy products.

I wait for her at the end of an aisle stuffed with odds and ends. Camera film, poker chips, playing cards, lip balm. I look up when I get the feeling that somebody is staring at me. On the other side of the window, Sadie is climbing into her dilapidated Ford Escort. I catch the outline of Ansel. He's blond and seems tall. Rain streams down the window. I can't see his face. Sadie isn't looking at me. Her head is turned so she can see behind her and back out. But I can catch enough of her face to realize that she's laughing. She's happy with Ansel. Happy without me.

Maybe she doesn't want to fix things between us. Maybe my friendship isn't that much of a loss. Sadie pulls out of her spot and onto the road, and I'm not okay. I feel anxious. I look around to see who is watching me. Nobody is paying any attention. Lightning rips through the sky again in a line so thick and jagged that it spawns a dozen branches.

I reach out and grab a package of red Bicycle playing cards. I put them in my coat pocket. I've never stolen from my father's store. Even as I'm doing it, something inside of me feels uncertain. But the act of taking the cards calms me. It feels good to have them.

"Molly, are you ready?" my mother asks. Maybe if she hadn't called to me at this exact moment I would have put them back. But her voice interrupts any further contemplating, and so I take the path of least resistance. I mean, I have the cards, so I keep the cards.

"I'm set," I say. I go to my mother and surrender my icecream pints. My father takes them and sets them in the bag.

"Heard you're not feeling well," he says.

Concerned about my date, I downplay everything. "I got overheated in practice."

"Well, cool down and take it slow. I'll try to be home early," he says.

I doubt that's true. I take our bag so my mother doesn't have to carry it, and we dart out of the Thirsty Truck and flee to the shelter of the green Galant.

"I think it's cute that you want to ask your date with ice cream," my mom says.

"Don't say it's cute," I say. "You make me feel like I'm twelve."

"Time is going by so fast," my mom says.

"It's going by normal speed," I say. "It just feels fast because in three months you're having a baby."

A baby. I can't believe it. Diapers. Colic. Bottles. What will our lives look like then? I reach over and turn on the radio, and a sad and familiar sound floats through the car. A saxophone.

"You want to listen to jazz?" I ask, assuming the radio accidentally ended up on this station. My mom usually enjoys soaking up talk radio shows. People calling in about difficult to diagnose car issues. Smart local people discussing topical events.

"Who doesn't like a little jazz?" my mom says.

I don't argue. I listen to the sweeping melody lines; they meander and march, and I can't help but think of Henry.

"Does your friend ever play shows in town?" my mom asks.

"No, not much," I say.

There aren't a lot of venues for jazz in Idaho Falls. But Henry has played a few times with two friends in coffee shops. One plays bass. The other drums. Henry says the manager always tells their trio to play more quietly. Sometime soon, if things don't feel too weird between us, I hope to make it to one of their infrequent gigs.

The music ends and the DJ tells us that we just listened to Dizzy Gillespie play a song called "I Remember Clifford," which was written by Benny Golson for his friend Clifford Brown, a genius trumpet player from the fifties who died at twenty-five in a car crash.

Rain continues to pound down over us, and my mother flips the windshield wipers to a faster speed.

"That's so freaking sad," I say.

"But it's a beautiful song," she says.

My window is starting to fog up. I use my finger to wipe a spot clear. "In a sad way."

"Do you want to change the station?"

I shake my head; we're almost home. "No. I like this."

SIX

Saturday, October 5

When I wake up, it's past eight o'clock, but I still feel tired. Is my life that exhausting? I think back to yesterday. Yes. It is. I hear my mother walking down the hall.

"Are you up yet?" she calls.

"Somewhat," I say.

She opens my door. She looks like she's been up a while. She's dressed and her hair looks nice, like she's ready to go out.

"If Joy calls, you should put her through," I say. "And if Tate calls, put him through. But if Ruthann calls, tell her I'm still sleeping."

"I don't have time for that," she says. "You need boots for your trip. I'm off to get them right now."

She walks into my room carrying her purse.

"Can't I just wear normal shoes?" I ask.

"You might run into problems with the stirrups."

I push off my covers and climb out of bed. "I think I'll be just fine. We're not going extreme horseback riding. We're just walking along a path."

"I had a dream last night. I gave birth on the bus again," she says.

My mother has been having weird pregnancy dreams for weeks. But I don't see how this is connected to boots.

"Was I in your dream?" I ask. "And was I wearing boots?

She shakes her head. "I wasn't prepared for the birth. Nobody was. Not me. Not the doctor. Not the bus driver."

It's unclear what triggers the bus pregnancy dreams. But each one is nearly identical. Except the number of people on board the bus varies with each dream.

"Did anybody help you this time?" I ask.

"Just the doctor," she says.

There is probably a person capable of psychoanalyzing this scenario. But this early in the morning, I'm in no shape to do it.

"It's just a dream," I say, trying to reassure her. "You don't even ride the bus."

She nods. "I know. I'm not actually afraid that I'm going to give birth on a bus. I just wonder if it means anything."

She can't be serious. "It doesn't," I say, pointing my finger at her to drive this point home.

"I love having an introspective and intelligent daughter," my mom says, walking to my door. "My friend Donna has a pair of boots that will fit you. I'm rushing there now."

How her dream triggered a boot crisis I'm still not quite sure.

The phone rings, but I'm afraid to answer it. "Wait! Before you go, can you answer that? And remember, if it's Ruthann, I'm not here."

"I'm not going to lie for you," my mother says. She leaves my room to answer the phone and calls down the hallway, "It's Tate."

Once I know it's him, I pick up the phone beside my bed.

Me: I've got it, Mom. You can hang up.

Tate: Just making sure that you've recovered.

Me: Yes. Fully.

Tate: Great. We'll swing by at ten.

Me: Should I pack a lunch?

Tate: We've got that covered.

Me: You don't even want me to bring an extra banana or something?

What's wrong with me? Why am I trying to force extra bananas into the car?

Tate: Feel free to bring a banana if you want a snack for the drive or something.

Me: Um, maybe I'll bring some trail mix.

Tate and I wrap up our awkward conversation and I hang up the phone. I have a talent for adding awkwardness to any situation. My mother has returned to the doorway. It feels like she's judging my telephone abilities with guys.

"Don't be nervous," she says. "He likes you."

Those words bring me to life. Because she's right. Tate likes me, and I have an amazing day ahead of me! Why am I worried about being awkward? Then I realize my mother is standing in the room. "I thought you were going to Donna's."

"I can't find the car keys."

"All right," I say. I am always helping my mother find her car keys. "Let me relive where you may have put them."

As I make my way to the kitchen, I pass the freezer and pull out a pint of the red velvet ice cream. My mother tags behind me.

"What are you doing?" she asks.

"After our horse trip I'm going to bring Tate back here and ask him to the dance. I need to get the ice cream ready."

I set the ice cream on top of the toaster oven and crank it to the medium heat setting.

"Why do you want to melt it?" my mother asks. "Is that some sort of fad these days? Eating melted ice cream?"

When my mother uses words like *fad* it makes her sound so old.

"I need to bury a note in the bottom. That's how he's going to know that I'm asking him to the dance." I crank the heat even higher. "So I need to scoop it out and repack it."

"Clever," my mom says. "But what about the keys?"

My dad enters the kitchen and grabs some bread.

"Wait," I tell him. "I'm using the toaster to melt my ice cream."

"You can't eat ice cream for breakfast," he says.

I spot the keys on the counter tucked behind a pile of our junk mail. I hand them to her. "Mom," I say, "can you explain the ice cream to him? I need to shower! And thanks for going to Donna's!"

"I'm headed to the store," my dad says. "Don't you have any equestrian questions for me before I leave?"

My father doesn't know that much about horses. I'm certain. But instead of racing down the hallway like a madwoman to get ready, I give my dad a quick hug and say, "I do. How do you make a horse go blazingly fast?"

My father tenses up a little, and I release him. "You don't," he says.

In his heart I know he'd rather I stayed home, so I probably shouldn't antagonize him, but I can't help it.

"I'm kidding," I say.

Then I race to get ready. Why didn't I get up earlier? I want to look perfect and amazing. Also, I want it to look like I didn't try hard at all.

After my shower I start setting out clothes. My focus isn't functionality. I want to look cute. Jeans? No. Too pedestrian. My black pants with all the pockets? They make my legs look so long. And they're tight in the butt in a way I think guys like. Pants decided. Do I need a coat? Yes. Mountains can be frigid. I hear the phone ring. Ugh. I am not going to talk to Ruthann. Considering how things are going, I should quit that stupid squad. High school shouldn't be this much drama. I should be enjoying myself. Being a triangle point isn't that important. So I'd get my picture taken and be featured on a news blog for a day. Am I going to put that on a job application? Will it matter when I'm thirty?

My father stands in the doorway holding the phone. I'm surprised he hasn't left yet. "I am not taking that call," I say. "I'm avoiding somebody." I say the last part in a whisper. I'm convinced that it's Ruthann. She wants to sabotage my date. I know it.

My father covers the receiver. "It's some guy named Henry."

A burst of excitement rushes through me. "Really?" I don't reach out for the phone. I'm not sure I want to talk to him. You can't jerk girls around like that. Melka or me. It's not fair. Henry doesn't deserve my attention right now. I'm doing something else.

"I don't want to take it," I say. "Can you tell him that I'll call him back?"

"Why? Is he bothering you?" my dad asks.

Oh, no. Did Henry hear my dad say that? "Tell him I'm getting ready to go horseback riding. I'll call him when I get back."

My father looks suspicious. But I want Henry to be a little disappointed. He should have considered that I might not take his calls before he made out with me and got back together with Melka.

From the hallway I hear my father explaining that I'm getting ready for a day trip to Wyoming. I hope Henry understands that I'm going out with Tate. Let Henry Shaw feel what I felt. He's coming in second. How does that feel? Nobody wants to think of himself as the runner-up.

"I'm officially gone now," my dad yells from the kitchen. "I love you."

"Ditto!" I call.

"Uh-oh!" he calls. "We've got a problem. But it's not huge."

I hope he's joking.

"Hopkins got out," my dad says.

Traditionally, Hopkins escapes less than five times a year, during spring and summer months, when our neighborhood squirrels are most active. Apart from that, he accepts his indoor imprisonment. I have no idea what inspired him to bolt today. This fall, our neighborhood squirrel population has dropped to nearly nil.

"He'll find his way home," I yell. He always does. I'm sympathetic toward him. If I were an indoor cat, I think I'd break out every now and again too.

I go back to my room and look at myself in the mirror. I do not love this shirt. But I need layers. Maybe I can cover it up. No. I want a cotton shirt. Pink goes well with black. The shirt I really want is in the basement, draped over my mother's old-fashioned collapsible drying rack.

I don't know why I feel so rushed. It's not like Tate is going to be here in ten minutes. But maybe he'll be early. I quicken my pace and go downstairs. As I'm changing shirts I hear a car tearing up our gravel driveway. Then I hear the sound of footsteps racing up the sidewalk. I stand on a box so I can look out our sunken window. Who's at my house? Is Tate early? Did Henry come over? No way! I can see Ruthann's shoes.

She pounds hard on the metal screen door. Our doorbell is broken, so even if she's trying to ring it, her efforts are futile.

"Molly Weller, open the door!"

How can she possibly know I'm here? I back away from the window and sit down next to the collapsible drying rack.

"When Tate comes by to pick you up, I want to talk to him."

She's nuts. That's not happening.

She opens the creaky screen and pounds on our wood door. Her fists may be small, but they're very powerful. Once, I saw her crumple a half-full soda can like it was made out of air.

"I just passed your mom and dad on my way over. You weren't in either car. I know you're home. Open up."

Wow, she's so observant. I want to point out that I could have been in either car, fully reclined or squished inside the trunk, but that would require me to reveal myself. Maybe that's Ruthann's master plan. Maybe she's trying to smoke me out of my hole. I duck my head down.

"Open this door or I will sideline you on the drill team forever!" she says.

I don't move.

"I'm serious!"

I know she's serious, and I consider moving. But then I reconsider.

"Molly Weller, I refuse to be treated this way."

I figure she'll stick around for a few more minutes, blow off some steam, and then I'll pretend like this never happened.

"God, is that you, Molly? In your basement? Hiding underneath your mom's drying rack?"

I look up. Standing inside my window well, bending over to look through the dirt-crusted glass, is the terrifying face of Ruthann Culpepper.

"What are you doing? Have you lost it? Are you having a breakdown?" Ruthann says.

I don't know what to do. I shake my head. Because I'm not having a breakdown. Not yet.

"Come let me in. We need to talk."

Oh my god. This is worse than a home invasion. She is not going to ruin my date. It will not happen. I will call whomever I need to prevent this.

"Leave now, or I'll call nine-one-one!" I yell.

Wow, did I actually just yell that? I sound so hard-core. *Too hard-core.* Ruthann smashes her hand against the window, tying to make a clear spot, but it just muddies the glass.

"Are you mental or something? You can't call 911 over this."

Before I can argue either for or against my terrible idea of calling 911, Ruthann starts screaming. I scream too. For no real reason.

"It's biting me!" she yells.

I stop screaming. Something's biting her? That's weird. Maybe it's my neighbor's dog, Ralph. He's supposed to be on a chain, but he's an American bulldog, and when it comes to escaping fences and collars, that pooch has proven himself to be a regular Houdini. I decide that it's not appropriate to let a fellow human being be mauled by my neighbor's dog, so I hurry upstairs to help. I grab our mop as a defensive weapon and swing open the door.

Once I see what's actually happening, I feel slightly relieved. Hopkins has leaped onto Ruthann's back. He's sunk his claws into her and is trying to bite the nape of her neck. But because of the thick expanse of her hair, there's no way Hopkins can land a good bite.

"Hopkins," I cry, "stop!"

But Hopkins doesn't release his grip. Finally, Ruthann grabs hold of his gray tail and yanks on it, dislodging him from her back. Hopkins lands hard on the ground. He stands, shakes his stunned head a couple of times, and attempts to trot to me. But Ruthann intercepts him with a quick scoop.

"Your cat is a total animal," Ruthann says.

"Well, that's not news. All cats are animals."

"I'm not giving him back."

"You have to. A cat is considered property. That's theft."

"He attacked me. I need to take him to get tested. To make sure he didn't give me any diseases."

I'm tempted to tell her that I consider her a disease. Ruthann turns and walks to her car, keeping Hopkins tucked under her arm.

"Ruthann, if you take my cat, I'll call the police. Seriously."

She smiles at me, not a happy smile, but a sinister one. She tightens her grip on Hopkins, and he whines.

"Stop it," I say.

"Yeah, it sucks to have people mess with your life, doesn't it?"

"I never messed with your life. Put down my cat. You're hurting him."

"No," she says, whacking him on the head with her open palm.

She shouldn't have done that. Then it happens: Hopkins

reacts and becomes a claw-crazy beast. He digs into the pale skin of her arm and sinks his teeth into her thumb.

"You shit!" she screams, flinging him away.

Hopkins darts toward me, and I open the door for him. He rushes inside and doesn't stop running. I can hear his claws clicking across the kitchen's linoleum floor. For caution's sake, I flip the latch and lock the screen door.

"Your cat is a menace to society. I'm going to call the authorities and report this incident." Ruthann rubs at her scratches.

"You can't do that. You hit him!"

"I'd kiss your mangy beast good-bye. By the time I'm through telling my side, they'll have no choice but to put that cat down."

"It wasn't Hopkins's fault. I should call PETA. They loathe animal abusers."

"I'm not afraid of PETA. And animal control will put your cat down. If an animal viciously attacks a person, it's sayonara, pussycat."

"You won't. You can't."

"Oh, now that I don't have a job anymore I've got loads of free time. Your cat is as crazy as you are. Its first attack was totally unprovoked."

She sort of has a point. Why did Hopkins jump her like she was a gargantuan rat? Ruthann tosses her head, and one possibility hits me.

"It was an innocent mistake. Your hair looks like a pack of squirrels."

She looks back at me and scowls.

"What?"

I realize she has taken that as an insult.

"Game on, Molly Weller. Game on."

She raises her hand like she's going to flip me the bird, but she doesn't. Bird-flipping must be slightly below her etiquette level. She gets in her car and pulls out of my driveway, and I feel sick. Hopkins slinks back into the room and weaves between my legs. I shut the front door and pick him up. I kiss the top of his head between his ears.

"What were you thinking?" I ask him.

Hopkins lifts his front paw and licks at its underside. He concentrates on a tuft of fur growing between the pads of his third and fourth toes. When he realizes that I'm staring at him, he stops and looks up at me. I'm holding him like a baby and he doesn't like that. He squirms and I let him fall. Hopkins winds around the love seat, taking the long way back to his food dish.

It's hard to savor the joy of Tate and his Moroccan tan's imminent arrival while facing the potential euthanizing of my cat. Love and death don't go together. They just don't. I take the ice cream off the toaster and dump it into a bowl. Then I take a piece of paper and write my name as legibly and sexily as possible: *Molly Weller*. After covering it in clear packing tape, I place it in the bottom of the pint. Using a black pen, I write the instructions on the inside of the lid: *You'll have to eat it all if you want to go to the Sweetheart Ball with* . . . I hope after he reads it he doesn't hesitate with his answer. I imagine one word falling out of his mouth over and over: *Yes. Yes. Yes.*

seven

After putting the ice cream back in the freezer and reassuring myself eighteen times that Ruthann can't kill my cat, I am still freaked out that this might actually happen. The stress inside me continues to build. Tate will be here any minute and my mother isn't back yet. My mind won't stop, and begins to play a motion picture of my future. After killing Hopkins, Ruthann kicks me off the squad. I'm isolated. Rejected. Alone. I consider dropping out of high school. Breathe. Breathe. Breathe. A mountain getaway with my long-term crush should scream ROMANCE, not ANXIETY.

I try my hardest to put the Hopkins fear in a box. Then I go to my bedroom and fluff my hair for the twentieth time and make sure that I've got breath mints in my purse. Some things in life are beyond my control, but my breath is not one of those things. If I do kiss Tate, I want it to be like my kiss with Henry. When his lips met mine, everything in the world dissolved except for us. And then it was as if we were collapsing into each other. It was so amazing. I think about it. And think about it. I really need to stop thinking about it.

When I hear my mother pull into the garage, I'm relieved, but also worried. I don't want to tell her about the Hopkins situation. I return to the kitchen. Addressing the Hopkins situation might unhinge me all over again. I'm not going to bring it up. But when my mother enters the house carrying my boots, she looks upset. She must know.

"I've already heard," she says. "Judy Culpepper called my cell."

"Can we talk about it after my date?" I say.

"She claims that Hopkins committed an unprovoked attack against her daughter," she says.

I guess we are going to talk about it before my date.

"What are we going to do?" I ask.

She sets her purse down on the counter and hands me the boots. They look like they've got cow crap on them.

"I told her we'd pay for any medical expenses."

I shake my head. "All she has is a few stupid scratches."

"Really? On the message her mother said that Hopkins severely bit her thumb."

"She squeezed him too tightly. And then she hit him! And then she tried to steal him. She's crazy!" My face feels hot, and I'm shouting.

"Don't yell at me. This isn't my fault. You're the one who dropped Sadie and picked Ruthann, out of all the possible friends in the area."

I don't want to talk about Sadie, so I focus on Ruthann. "I didn't know she was crazy," I say.

"They usually don't wear signs."

Hopkins doesn't like all this hubbub. He walks into the room and then leaves.

"We'll talk it over with your father."

"She wants to have him euthanized."

My mother rolls her eyes. "I doubt it will come to that."

Except for using the word *doubt*, she sounds pretty certain. This calms me. I sit and slide the boots on one at a time. They're snug, but I think they're supposed to be. My mother reaches down and brushes my bangs off my forehead. This is my chance to open up and tell her a little bit about what's going on with Joy and Ruthann. And fill her in on the nut shop story. The firing. But I don't.

"Thanks," I say. "These feel great."

We both hear Tate as he pulls into the driveway.

"Go and enjoy yourself," my mom says.

"I will," I say. "And don't let anything happen to the ice cream. The one on the right is the one I'm using to invite him to the dance. It's ready to roll."

When Tate comes to the door, I am mostly filled with excitement. I can't help but think about Hopkins and Ruthann. It sort of feels like it was all just part of some terrible movie that I barely finished watching.

"Nice boots," he says.

I look at them again and still think they look a little covered in cow crap.

"Thanks," I say.

We force some small talk with my mom and then we're finally on our way. I'm on my date. The one I've been looking forward to for weeks. Me. Tate. And a long horse ride through Wyoming. Forget Henry. I've got a better love story unfolding right in front of me.

"I'm Denise," a petite brunette in the passenger seat says as I climb into the backseat. "I think I've seen you at the juice bar."

"Yeah," I say. "I'm Molly."

"And I'm Wyatt," Tate's brother says. "I'm the oldest person in this car, and you should come to me for all factual information."

"Okay," I say, laughing a little.

"Don't ask him anything," Tate says.

"Here's something you might not know," Wyatt says. "It's a fact that Tate's favorite pizza topping is artichoke hearts."

"Interesting," I say. I can't tell if he's kidding or not.

"And it's a fact that Tate wins every potato sack race at family reunions because he cheats."

"I don't cheat," Tate says. "I'm fast. Even inside a bag."

"And it's a fact that his favorite sport is riding a water weenie behind our family boat."

"That is not my favorite sport," Tate says. "Football is my favorite sport. Basketball is a close second."

"But it's so hard to play that game while riding the weenie," Wyatt says.

"Okay," Denise says. "Let's stop talking about weenies."

I am relieved that Denise is here.

"I brought my Magic Eight Ball," Denise says. "Let's ask it questions."

My mind leaps to Hopkins. Is it weird to ask a Magic 8 Ball a question about my cat?

"Me first," Tate says.

Ooh. I'm curious to know what Tate thinks about. "Are we going to skunk Skyline?"

They're the rival football team. Tate is a running back. I guess it makes sense that his mind would be totally preoccupied with sports.

"*Most certainly!*" Denise squeals. "Okay. Me next. Should I go to Belize now or wait until next year, when I have more money?"

"What does it say?" I ask.

"*Without a doubt,*" Denise says. "Does that even make sense?"

I consider telling her that you can't ask a two-part question. But I don't. If she owns a Magic 8 Ball, she should know how it works.

"You go, Molly," Denise says.

I'm nervous. I don't want to ask a lame question. What I really want to ask is either about the fate of my cat or the fate of my heart, and both of those seem out of bounds, like the exact wrong question to ask in public. Instead, a random question pops out of my mouth.

"What are the chances that I'll fall off my horse?" I say.

"Zero," Tate says. "If you hold on to the reins."

"Don't focus on falling," Wyatt says. "That's a pessimist's game."

"Don't give her a hard time," Denise says. "She's allowed to ask the ball anything she wants. It's the rule of the ball."

Denise turns around and winks at me. She's so friendly. And easy to like. I bet she has a million friends.

"Once I had a dream that I fell off a horse," she says to me.

"Recently?" I ask.

"Nah. I don't have premonitions," Denise says. "I think the horse represented my PE teacher. He was such an ass. You can't ignore your dreams. They're unleashing stuff that we suppress all day. They mean shit."

"Yeah," I say. "Okay. That's my question. Um, I want to know if I'll fall off my horse."

"Expect the good outcome and it will find you," Wyatt says. "That's an old saying by a famous prophet. Or guru. Or something."

Denise looks at me again and rolls her eyes. "I'm going to ask it your question. Will Molly fall off her horse?" She lifts the ball and shakes it over her head. "*Outlook not so good.*"

"Cool," I say.

"Wait," Tate says. "I think that means you'll fall off."

"No," Denise says. "The outlook is not so good that she will fall off. You have to read the ball correctly."

"No," Wyatt says. "I think Tate is right. You played with

fate and now you better hold on tight. And not just with your hands. Hug with your thighs."

Denise laughs and turns toward the backseat. "Don't listen to him. You're going to be fine."

"I know," I say. "I'm wearing boots."

An hour goes by and Denise doesn't get tired of her Magic 8 Ball game. She asks it about China. Tate asks about upcoming NFL games. Wyatt asks it weird questions about tsunamis and volcanoes and alien landings in New Mexico. My mind wanders and I think about what it would be like to marry into this family. I'd be related to Wyatt. And probably Denise. Forever. We'd probably have to play this game all the time.

"We're almost there," Wyatt says. "You can almost smell that we're at Alpine heights."

I take a deep breath, but I don't smell that. As we turn off onto the mountain road I decide that I should ask the eight ball about Hopkins. "Will my cat survive his next battle?"

Denise peers into the ball. "*You may rely on it.*"

"Great news!" I feel authentic relief at that answer.

"You know, it's just a toy," Wyatt says. "If you're professionally fighting your cat, you shouldn't rely on the eight ball for advice."

"My cat's going through a metaphorical battle," I say.

"That's deep," Wyatt says. "I like the way you think."

Tate looks embarrassed. He bumps his shoulder against my shoulder in a flirty way, and I bump him back. It doesn't feel electric like it did with Henry. But it still feels pretty good. Henry or Tate. Henry or Tate. In a world where Melka doesn't exist and I had a choice, which one would I choose? Who would make the better boyfriend? I sort of want to run this by the Magic 8 Ball.

"We're here!" Denise yells, releasing her seat belt before we stop.

I look out the window. Good lord. Are those our horses? I am overwhelmed by feelings of eagerness, awe, and terror.

eight

I guess I'm not a fan of the horse after all. I mean, these look like they're on steroids or something. Tate tries to calm me down.

"They're more afraid of you than you are of them."

"Who said I'm afraid?" I ask.

"You haven't gotten out of the car yet."

I look at him and then I look around inside the car's immaculate backseat. He's right. It's time to exit the vehicle.

"I need to tell Wyatt something," Tate says, glancing over his shoulder. "I'll be right back."

Wyatt and Denise have already picked out their horses. I've decided that they're a mildly weird couple. And seated on their big, tan, glossy horses, they only look weirder. Tate and Wyatt talk, and I suck in deep breaths. It smells like a minty cough drop inside the car. It's the air freshener. I look between the front seats, at the dashboard. I see a plastic ladybug dangling from the cigarette lighter. Who knew air fresheners came in such cute packaging? I look back out the window. Nobody is watching. I reach forward and unloop the ladybug from the lighter's knob. Then I shove the plastic bug into my jacket pocket. I zip it closed.

When I look back at Tate and Wyatt I begin to grow concerned that they're planning something. But that's stupid. What could they be planning? Because Wyatt has the most riding experience, it was decided on the way up that he would ride the lead horse.

I watch that horse strike his front hoof against the ground, sort of like he's trying to dig into the earth and make a hole. Until now, I hadn't realized that horses had an innate desire to dig. I pictured them more as sleigh and carriage pullers.

Tate walks back to the car smiling. I know it's time for me to get out and join everybody. If I stay in the car any longer I'll look too weird to date. I open my door a crack.

I walk toward Tate and the horses. From the road, or inside my television, they have always seemed about my height, not this massive. In actuality, I only go up to a horse's tail. A man has already unloaded the towering animals from a trailer. He's saddled them and done whatever else you do to a horse before a person mounts it and rides it through the mountains.

"This is Peppa," says Tate, leading a white horse with black speckles toward me. "He'll be your horse. I'll be riding Salt." Salt is a black horse. Because I doubt cowboys have a sense of irony, clearly these horses have been misnamed.

"What are the names of their horses?" I ask, pointing to Wyatt and Denise. Their horses are both gargantuan and tan.

"Pickles and Ballerina."

I wonder if Wyatt renamed them for comic effect, or if these are their actual names.

"Who's riding Pickles?" I ask.

"Denise."

I look at my horse and can see right up its cavernous nostrils. Then it opens its mouth. Oh my god. I never realized that horses had such enormous teeth. I thought they were vegetarians and just ate grain. I take hold of Peppa's reins. He pulls his head back and whinnies.

"Horses can sense fear," Tate says.

I frown at my horse, hoping I'll be able to confuse him. Maybe he'll think I'm not afraid, but ticked off. We walk our horses over to Wyatt and Denise, who are already perched in their saddles.

"The air smells like a mountain," Denise says.

Of course, at that very moment, my horse releases a well-timed fart. Everybody looks at me. I look disapprovingly at Peppa's back end.

"Do you need help?" Tate asks, pointing to my saddle horn.

"I think I can do it."

I slip my boot into the stirrup and pull myself up off the ground. For some dumb reason, Peppa starts walking toward the brush, and I haven't even slung my leg over yet. I'm not even on him.

"Whoa!" I say.

Tate smiles as he watches me hoist myself onto my moving horse.

"Nice job, Lone Ranger," Wyatt says. "Last one down the trail owes the rest of us fifty bucks."

"Wyatt," Denise says. "Molly might not know that you're joking."

Does Denise think I'm developmentally challenged? I didn't really think I'd owe anybody fifty bucks. Denise keeps explaining how this is a joke.

"The horses are trained to follow each other single file, and you're the lead horse. Of course, Molly, you'll be the last one there."

"That's fine," I say. I hadn't expected my date to be a race.

"Now that we understand the equine mind, let's get this party started," Wyatt says. He lightly kicks his boots against Ballerina's side and she starts to move.

"We can give them a little leeway," Tate says. "We don't have to stick right at their heels."

But Peppa seems to want to follow them very closely. He's rushing to stay with the lead horse. Tate angles his horse across the path, blocking Peppa's progress.

"Once Ballerina is out of sight, he'll loosen up. He won't want to hurry."

"Okay."

Then Peppa releases an excruciatingly long fart. It's like my horse is part whoopee cushion.

"Do they feed them a pure bean diet?" I ask.

"Some horses are just gassier than others, I guess."

Tate makes Salt walk right next to Peppa. I don't think that they're used to walking shoulder to shoulder like this.

They seem to want to walk single file, like Denise said. But after a few minutes, they settle down. Tate is full of questions. He asks about Tigerettes.

"Why do you like it so much?" he asks.

I don't know why he assumes that I like it that much.

"I don't know," I say. "I want to be part of something. When high school is over I want to be able to look back and say, I did that."

"You really think ahead," Tate says.

I'm not quite sure how to take that comment. Is he judging me? There's nothing wrong with thinking ahead. High school will be over in two years. I'm not thinking that far ahead. "I want to get the most out of everything," I explain. "Life is for living." Ooh. That sounded cheesy. Why am I suddenly saying cheesy things?

"And that means being a Tigerette?" Tate asks.

"This year it does," I say defensively. It sounds like he hates our drill team. Which is not cool. He's an athlete. He should appreciate us.

I let Salt and Peppa walk in silence, their hooves clomping against the hard dirt trail.

We pass a thick bank of trees that have already dropped their fall leaves. Our horses mash over them. "I bet this place had gorgeous foliage."

"So you're a leaf peeper," Tate says in a joking voice.

"I would never use the word 'peeper' to describe myself," I say.

"I don't know. I like it. Peeper," Tate says. "I might start calling you that."

"I'm sixteen. You cannot start calling me Peeper. I won't allow it." I like that Tate is playful. But he's also more immature than I realized. Unlike Henry, who is considerably more mature than I realized. Why am I still thinking about Henry?

"I thought you were seventeen," Tate says.

"No, not until February."

"Seventeen's great. It's like the beginning of everything."

I've heard that about sixteen, eighteen, and twenty-one, but never seventeen.

"That's when things really started happening for me," he says.

It sort of sounds like he's talking about losing his virginity. Is that what he means? I guess seventeen is a reasonable age for that. I don't personally feel ready to be deflowered. It's always struck me as a good idea to hold on to that for as long as possible.

Tate steers Salt so close to my horse that his legs and my legs touch. From the corner of my eye, I see Tate reach for my thigh.

"Hey, Peeper, make Peppa stop."

I need to break him of this nickname as politely as I can. I pull back lightly on the reins and Peppa stands still. Salt has stopped, too. Tate leans over and slides his hand beneath my hair, setting it on the nape of my neck. I lean toward him and close my eyes. I think I smell ham. Or baloney. Finally, I will be able to compare his kisses to Henry's kisses. My lips actually tingle in anticipation. Then I realize something terrible. There's no way this can happen.

I'm leaning too far already and our lips aren't even close. Kissing on horseback, unless you're on the same horse, is essentially impossible.

"I can't," I say.

"Why?" he asks.

"I'll fall," I say.

He seems to believe me.

"Maybe at the end," I say.

"Maybe?" he asks.

"Most likely at the end," I say. My mind flashes to Henry and our make-out session. I really wish my mind would stop doing that.

Tate pulls away from me and sits up in his saddle.

"Wow," he says. "In addition to the pine trees I think I can smell eucalyptus."

I look down at the ground. The scent of the air freshener wafts out of my pocket the way the smell of baking bread escapes an oven. Taking it was a bad decision. At the first chance I have, I need to throw it into a bush and get rid of it.

Tate kicks Salt lightly in the side and makes a clicking sound with his mouth.

"We should get going," he says.

I nod and smile. Peppa clops along just fine for a bit. But then he starts trying to wander off into the brush again. Like maybe there's a fresh can of beans out there just waiting to be devoured.

"Come on," I encourage in a stern voice.

"You okay?" Tate asks.

Salt and Tate have pulled ahead of us quite a bit. I'm not panicked or anything, but I don't want Peppa to start backtracking. I kick him lightly in the sides. He lowers his head to the ground and chomps off the head of a tuft of weeds.

"Kick him again," Tate says.

I try, but he wanders farther off the trail.

"Peppa, go back to the trail," I say.

Tate coaxes Salt off the trail.

"We're on our way," he says.

But he's at least a basketball court away, and I'm starting to feel nervous. I think Tate can sense this.

"You're fine," he says.

Right as he says that, I hear somebody shaking a maraca. Peppa tries to go in reverse, but the sound grows louder. Then, suddenly, Peppa is standing on his back legs. His front legs look like they're trying to climb a ladder into the sky. There's no way for me to stay in the saddle. As I'm tumbling off the back end of the horse, I can see something moving on the ground. It looks like a piece of rope. It flashes. Then it's gone. I feel pain. First in my butt and then in my head. And then I don't feel anything.

nine

When I wake up, I'm alone. I'm lying in the brush and there's a white horse tied to a woody shrub. Wait. That's my horse. That's Peppa. I try to lift my head, but it hurts. I reach up and touch it, and my hand gets wet. I pull my hand away and look at it. It's covered in blood. Crap. It's my blood. I've hit my head. Where's Tate? I rest my head back in the dirt.

How much blood have I lost? I remember reading somewhere that nothing bleeds like a head wound. I think I'm supposed to apply pressure to it. Again, I reach up to touch the cut. This time I realize that I'm not touching my head. Something is tied around my head. I can feel buttons. And a pocket. I pull on a piece of loose fabric and lift up the sleeve of Tate's shirt. Wow, if I wasn't bleeding to death by myself in the wilderness, I would think that gesture was so sweet.

I let the sleeve fall to the ground. I can't believe this is happening. God, my butt feels like it has a rock wedged deep beneath the skin. It feels like it's swelling. Did I land on a patch of thistle? I can't find a comfortable position. It's too painful to even try to shift the weight of my body, so I lie flat on my back in the dirt.

As I breathe, I notice something rising and falling on my chest. It's a small rock. When I push it off, a piece of paper flies away. Using my right hand, I smash the paper flat to the ground, then drag it back to me. As I raise it up, I see that it's a note. But it's hard to read. Things are blurry. How hard did I hit my head? It's from Tate. I make out his signature and take a few breaths. As I squint, trying to make the words come into focus, pain pumps through me. I manage to get through the note anyway.

Molly,
I've gone to get help. You fell and hit your head. Peppa is tied to a bush. Back soon.
    Love, Tate

Holy crap! He used the word love. I know it probably doesn't mean anything. He was probably just in a hurry and that's how he signs all of his notes. Weird. He doesn't love me. Does he? I read it again. Then everything is so blurry that I have to put the note away. I retrieve the rock and set it right on my chest again, where Tate left it. But I keep holding the note. I close my eyes. I bet he'll be here with help really soon.

We're not that far away from the trailhead. I bet whoever comes to get me will be able to drive a truck right to this spot. I mean, people get hit on the head all the time. It's not like I've fallen down an inaccessible cliff and broken all my bones. I try to calm myself down by telling myself that the more I relax, the better I'll feel. But, that's a lie. I'm in agony.

I open my eyes again. That's when I remember it. The ladybug. I need to get rid of the air freshener. Nobody can find that in my pocket. That discovery would be the worst thing that has ever happened to me. Tate would learn that I was a thief. He wouldn't like me anymore. He might even hate me. Or think I was crazy. He'd never trust me. I try to open my pocket. I can't. Opening the zipper feels impossible. My fingers won't bend. I can't make myself move the way I need to move. Of all the ways to get caught. A ladybug air freshener? How humiliating.

At least I'm not alone. I have a horse to keep me company. I look in Peppa's direction. He's eating a patch of grass. I sure wish I could've fallen in a soft patch of grass. My butt would feel a whole lot better. Out of the corner of my eye, I see something small and black on the ground. It's near my face and moving closer to me. It's a tick! Wait. It's a beetle.

I press my lips closed and feel it crawl across my mouth. I bet it has mandibles. Beetles bite, right? Indiscriminately? It walks right up to the cave of my right nostril. Am I going to have a beetle stuck in my nasal cavity? Is that even possible? It kills me to move, but I turn my head quickly and the beetle races away from my nose and traipses across my cheek, tickling me in a horrible way. I jerk my head the other direction. The blurred beetle climbs off me and crawls through the dirt, out of view.

Unless Tate returns within the next couple of minutes, more bugs will be crawling on me. I need to come up with ways to keep them off. How? My mind isn't able to think of any ideas. I close my eyes and open them again. The sun is up. At least I'm not cold. Wait. I think I have an idea. I will kill all future bugs by swatting them with the rock on my chest. I reach up and take hold of the rock.

I notice that my fingers tingle. My toes too. Even my lips. And they don't tingle like in the way when Tate almost kissed me. It's like something is seriously wrong. I bet I've injured my spinal cord. I bet its juices are leaking inside of me and I'm going to lose feeling in all of my extremities. I'm going to be a paraplegic. Maybe even a quadriplegic. I never should have told Tate that I liked horses. I glare at Peppa like I want him to die. He doesn't even look at me. Then he takes a foul-smelling dump downwind of me. Thanks.

The Magic 8 Ball was wrong. I *did* fall off my stupid horse.

I close my eyes and try to forget about the tingling and the bleeding and the awful smell of hot, fresh dung. I fall inside of myself to a place like sleep, but it's not quite sleep, because I'm in constant pain. I feel other bugs tripping across my hands and face. I don't have the energy to hit them with the rock. They feel small. I don't think they're biting me. Normally, I'd be freaked out, but it's almost a relief, because at least I can still feel them.

I hear an engine. Is it my imagination? No; why would I imagine an engine? I open my eyes, and the whole world, even the soft blue sky, is blurred. I don't try to angle my head to see a truck. My head aches. Tate is at my side. I can feel him holding my hand. He's with two guys I've never seen before, with puffy gray beards. Wait. There's only one guy. I'm totally seeing double.

"It's not too bad," he tells Tate. "We'll drive her to the hospital."

Tate gives my hand three quick squeezes.

"You're going to be just fine," the man says. "I've seen a lot of injuries over the years, and your head wound is small potatoes."

I feel a little offended by this comment. I mean, he's marginalizing my head wound. Then this guy yells for some other guy named Darrell to take Peppa and get Wyatt and Denise. He tells Darrell to bring them to the hospital.

"Don't I need an ambulance?" I ask.

My mouth feels different; it's slick with spit. It takes effort for me to speak.

"It'd take longer to wait for one," he says.

"Actually, I called 911 at your office. I gave them directions to the trailhead," Tate says.

I hear sirens approaching. I'm so relieved. I don't know who this two-headed bearded guy is, but clearly he's no medical doctor. I've only taken two semesters of biology and I'm certain my injuries aren't "small potatoes." Even the way the paramedics slam their doors and run to me gives me more comfort than my original rescuer.

"What's her name?" the first paramedic asks.

"Molly Weller," Tate says.

"Molly, do you know what day it is?"

I focus all my energy to answer. "Saturday."

"Do you know where you are?"

Again, an answer takes all my energy. "In the dirt."

"How did you get in the dirt?"

I can't keep answering these questions. "My horse dumped me."

"Does your head hurt?"

"Yes."

"Do you hurt anywhere else?"

I know I should say that my butt hurts, but I'm so tired. And that's embarrassing. And really, isn't a head wound far more serious than a butt wound? I don't tell the paramedic.

"My head," I mumble.

"We're going to put you on this board and lift you into the ambulance. I want you to stay awake."

I blink, and hope that the paramedic understands that this means I heard him and will try to stay awake. I reach up and grab the note, and the rock tumbles off of me. When they roll me onto the board, I moan.

"You're okay," the bearded man says.

He has no idea whether or not I'm okay. I'm the one inside my injured body.

The paramedics load me into the ambulance, and Tate tells me that he'll be riding in front with the driver. He squeezes my hand.

On the drive to the hospital, the medic spends a lot of time dealing with my head wound. He takes off Tate's make-shift bandage and dresses it properly. After he's cleaned my wound and applied fresh bandages, the medic sits back and takes a deep breath. There's a lot of beeping machines back here. I feel like I'm tucked inside a metal lunch box. My fingers are so tingly that I loosen my grip on the note, and it falls. The paramedic picks it up and hands it back to me.

"'Love Tate,'" he says. "Sounds serious."

"It's our first date," I say. My voice is barely a whisper.

"You'll remember this one for a long time."

I nod. And close my eyes.

"Stay awake, Molly," the medic says. His voice is stern.

I don't think I can stay awake.

"Does your girlfriend have any preexisting medical conditions?" the paramedic yells.

He sounds so worried.

"I don't think so," Tate shouts. "She might be recovering from the flu."

No, I want to tell them. *That's not right. Not the flu. Ruthann. I am recovering from Ruthann.*

"Molly, I need you to be a good girl and stay awake for me."

I feel the medic lightly slap my cheeks. He's not trying to hurt me. He wants to reach me. I know this because I'm falling somewhere inside of myself again. Falling to a place deeper than I've ever fallen before.

"Molly! Be good," he says. "Stay with me."

Be good? Stay with you? I don't think I can. Things feel out of my hands. The word *good* ricochets through me. I'm not good. Just ask Sadie. Or Joy. Or the ladybug air freshener. *Be good? Stay with you?* I haven't been good for a long time. How can I start now?

The paramedic may still be yelling at me, but I can't hear him anymore. The sirens have faded away too. Maybe we've arrived at the hospital and everybody is being very quiet. But why would they do that? I'm on the verge of letting out a big breath. I don't feel like myself anymore. My body feels light and feathery. Like I've been turned into air. I don't think I'm even in my body anymore. It feels like I'm rising, floating above everything. Myself. The paramedic. Tate. The ambulance. Wyoming. Everything.

ten

$\mathcal{A}$m I in the principal's office? The painted wood paneling on the walls reminds me of Mrs. Milmer's sparsely lit cave, where, depending on the student, she either doles out a punishment or reward. (My sophomore year, along with Sadie, I received a certificate for perfect attendance.) But I don't see any pictures of Mrs. Milmer's big-nosed, broad-shouldered, dark-haired family. And there aren't any degrees from her alma mater hanging on the walls.

In front of me is a large oak desk. It sure looks like Mrs. Milmer's. A scattering of papers is flung across its surface. Clearly, whoever owns this desk is overworked and overwhelmed. The weird thing is, I don't see a single pen. Only papers. I stand up and sneak a glance at the mounds of desk work. To avoid being intrusive, I don't touch anything. I'm looking to see if my name is on any of them. I mean, why am I even here? The papers all look blank.

I know I shouldn't be snooping. I'm about to sit back down when I see the corner of a nameplate. The sign says LOUISE DAVIS. Do I know a Louise Davis? Is she my dentist?

No, that's Louise David, DDS. Isn't it? None of this makes sense, and so I sit down in my wooden chair.

I have no idea what I'm wearing. Is it a bathrobe? How did I wind up dressed in a bathrobe? I wouldn't leave the house like this. Maybe if I focus on the last place I was I can figure out how I got here. My mind is blank. If I stay alone in this room without any answers for one more minute, I am going to lose my mind. That's how panicked I feel. I need to see someone I know. My mother. I need to see my mother.

I keep searching the wood-paneled walls for answers. There isn't a single window in this room. And there aren't any doors. No. This is impossible. Maybe I've already lost my mind. Maybe I'm in a lockdown area. A clock ticks behind me. I turn and look. Wow. It's not one single clock. It's a wall of clocks. Row after row of round ticking time-pieces the size of dinner plates. There's at least a hundred. They must be keeping track of every time zone on the planet. Maybe even beyond.

"Molly, I'm sorry to leave you suspended."

A woman with dark gray hair stands behind the desk wearing a smart navy blue suit. She's not my dentist. And she's not my principal. Where did she even come from? Was she underneath the desk?

"Are you Louise Davis?" I ask.

Her eyes are gray too, and they widen in surprise when I call her by her name.

"Oh, you found the placard."

I nod.

"For a minute I thought you were already tuning in to all the frequencies now available to you. You have a lot of gifts to explore."

I look around the room, hoping to see presents. Maybe this is a surprise party. Except, my birthday isn't until February. Wait, is it February?

"Molly, please listen very closely to what I'm about to say."

She walks from behind her desk toward me. For her age, I think she's quite slim and attractive, and I hope when I get older that I can look as good as she does.

"I am Louise Davis. I will be your intake officer concerning all matters of the soul. You are in the process of crossing over. I will be with you for your entire journey."

This doesn't make much sense to me. I'm not a soul. I'm a person. I'm in high school. Why do I have an intake officer? Wait, I remember. I fell off a horse. I'm in the hospital. Louise must be a nurse. I wonder why she isn't wearing scrubs and a name tag. Maybe it's common hospital lingo to refer to people as souls.

"Please sit. Due to your sudden passing, it will take a moment for everything to catch up with you."

"I'm already sitting."

"Right, right, I'm running behind."

Great. She's inept. I'm probably dealing with a flunked-out nurse. How can I tactfully get a different one?

"Shouldn't I be on a gurney? I have a head wound."

Louise reaches into her piles of paper like she's double-checking something.

"No, nobody crosses over on a gurney."

"How is that even possible? What kind of hospital is this?"

I realize for the first time that my head doesn't hurt. Or my butt. I mean, I'm able to sit in a wooden chair. To be honest, I feel rather pleasant all over. But I'm completely confused.

"Molly, this isn't a hospital."

"Then I'm in the wrong place. I was in an ambulance."

Louise shakes her head, and her no-nonsense bob swings a little.

"If this isn't a hospital, am I in some sort of clinic?" I shouldn't be. My parents have good health insurance.

"Molly, I'm sorry to inform you of this—it will most likely be catching up with you any second now—but you've died. You're in the process of crossing over from life to death. I'm Louise Davis, your intake counselor concerning all matters of the soul. I'll be helping you cross."

"You're repeating yourself. And I don't believe you."

Something is not right. Why is this woman lying to me? Oh my god. Maybe I've been abducted. I've heard stories about deranged infertile women who steal babies and children and teenagers. But never in a million years did I think I'd become a victim. How do I get out of here?

"Sometimes repetition helps it sink in. And you need to stop thinking about escape. You are exactly where you are supposed to be."

As I keep looking around the room, I notice that some things do appear weird and maybe somewhat otherworldly.

The clocks. The lack of an entrance. And windows. I mean, there's no light source, not even a lamp, but the room is lit well enough for me to see. Both Louise and I do seem pale and so do the ivory sofa and pine desk. We look thin, too, almost transparent. It's like everything in the room has been made out of thinly sliced pieces of bread. Even me.

"Why am I wearing a bathrobe?"

"I don't know." Louise glances down at the papers. "My mistake."

I look down again. I'm wearing black cotton pants and my favorite pink shirt. They were the clothes I was wearing during the accident. But I'm not wearing my borrowed boots. I just have on socks. This is so weird.

"I can't really be dead," I say.

Louise nods. "You are."

A variety of terrible feelings stampedes through me: panic, sadness, despair, surprise, alarm, confusion, denial. There is no way I'm dead. I don't know what it means to *be dead* or *cross over*. I've never read the Bible or been to church. I'm sixteen. How can I be dead? I was in an ambulance surrounded by a medical team. I was on my way to a hospital. People were helping me.

"But my head wound was small potatoes," I say.

"True," Louise says.

"So I might still pull through?" I ask, reaching for any thread of hope.

"No," Louise says in a very flat voice. "You died."

This answer triggers an even bigger stampede of terrible feelings. "Whoa," I hear myself say. "Whoa." Even though I really don't believe what I'm being told, I try to pull myself together by asking logical, anxiety-calming questions.

"Okay, Louise. Let's say that I am dead. Is this Heaven?"

Louise shakes her head. My mouth drops open, and if I had a body and was able to cry, I'd be openly weeping. This news is worse than being told that I am dead. Because apparently I didn't make it to Heaven. Which means I must be in the other place.

"No," I say. "This can't be happening!"

I do not deserve to die *or* be sent to Hell. I'm certain.

Louise jerks her head up and looks concerned. "Don't overreact before you know what's going on."

I walk to the clocks on the back wall. There aren't any numbers. They have words written on them. Names. People I know. Henry Shaw. Melka Klima. Tate Arnold. My parents. Before I can move closer and read more names, Louise intercepts me.

"Don't worry about the clocks," she says. "My job is to explain things as we go. We'll get to those soon enough."

The clocks seem important.

"Am I supposed to meet people at certain times?" I ask.

"No. No. No. Stop trying to figure it all out," Louise says. "Relax."

"There is no way that's happening," I say.

"The first step in this process is that we must review your death."

"Review my death?"

"Yes."

"How?"

"We have a special projection system. Follow me."

Follow her? Watch my own death? "I'm not sure I want to see that, Louise." I try to keep my voice polite, but really I'm shocked and disgusted by this arrangement.

"You must. It's required."

How can somebody force me to watch my own death? She can't. "I'm not going." I don't refuse to follow rules very often, but my gut tells me that I should stay where I am. What I'm being told is insane. And I don't have to follow insane rules. I just don't.

"Either you follow me right now, like a reasonable soul, or I will make you come."

Make me come? Who does this woman think she is? "Okay. You're going to have to make me come," I say.

Louise sighs and looks disappointed. "You're wasting time."

But if I really am dead, which I still don't totally believe, isn't time all I've got now?

"Follow me to the viewing room," she says.

I plan to stand still and resist all forward movement. Instead, a rope of energy wraps itself around me, constricting my arms and legs, and tugs me against my will through a wall. Then I'm in a long white hallway being dragged to the viewing room.

This must be a dream. There is no way this is happening. *Wake up! Wake up! Wake up!* Maybe I was knocked out with some sort of anesthesia that's making me dream freaky things.

"Once you watch your own death, you'll begin to accept

that your life has expired and you're about to start the next phase of your existence," Louise says.

The hallway goes on and on.

She continued, "If you hadn't resisted, and were coming along willingly, this would be a thrilling walk down memory lane. The hallway would illuminate important moments in your life. Have you heard the phrase, I watched my life pass before my eyes?"

"Yeah," I say. Dying didn't take away my intelligence.

"Well, you're missing that part," Louise says.

Is it this woman's job to make me feel worse than I've ever felt in my whole entire life?

"Do you want to experience that?" she finally asks.

I don't hesitate. "Yes." If I really am dead (which I'm not), and this is my last chance to see my life (which it can't be), then of course I want to experience that.

As soon as I say the word *yes*, the rope of energy releases its hold on me, giving me the power to move about freely. I slow my pace and watch the walls, hoping to see the movie of my life. But everything is still achingly white. The paint job is immaculate.

"Do I need to say something to make my memories appear?" I can't figure this out. I feel stunned. Shocked. Completely out of sorts.

"Be patient," Louise urges.

Once she says that, it happens. It's not a movie, as I thought it was going to be; my life arrives in photographs. I see pictures that I don't think my mother or anybody else actually took. Gold frames form around them and they cover the hallways top to bottom. There are so many. As I move past them, I'm overwhelmed by sensations that are frozen inside those moments. Approaching a picture of my family at the beach, I swear I can smell the ocean. And as I study a picture of my third birthday, I can taste the sweet chocolate frosting buttered to the roof of my mouth. With each step I take toward the viewing room, the photos show me growing older.

"I don't remember that day," I say, pointing to me sitting in a shopping cart. "I must have been four years old. What was special about that day?"

"Something you'll soon realize is that every day you were alive was a special day."

It might be possible that I am dead.

In one of the photographs, I'm playing with a yellow dog. I don't recall interacting with that dog. Ever. In another I'm riding my bicycle down the sidewalk in front of my grandma's house, alongside a row of her lush red geraniums. Seeing this stirs a sadness inside me that's so sharp the only way I can shake it is by trying to think logistically.

"So everybody gets their own long white hallway? And you have to swap the photos out for every death? And every dead person gets a counselor?" I convince myself that this will feel easier if I can figure out the system.

Louise stops walking and turns around. We're not even halfway down the hallway. She tilts her head and looks concerned. "What does it matter how it works for other people? You're the dead person being given the gift of an extensive memory lane. Live it again. Feel everything. Let yourself."

I nod at Louise like I get her point. But she doesn't understand that looking at the photos and inhabiting those memories feels just as bitter as it does sweet. As we reach the end of the wall, I see pictures so recent and familiar that it's hard to believe they're hanging in these frames.

"Somebody took a photo of breakfast?" I say. The picture shows the three of us last weekend eating pancakes; my mother and I are in our pajamas, and my father is dressed in his work clothes. It looks like I'm talking. I must be telling a joke, because both of my parents appear to be on the edge of laughter. And then there's a picture of me speaking angrily to Henry in the lunchroom over the garbage can. Energy whirls through me. That was this week. And now I'm dead. No way. The final picture is of me sitting on top of a stupid horse. Leaning in to kiss me, Tate appears happy and completely unaware of what's about to happen. Of course he looks this way. We're both completely unaware. Until my fall, we were both naive enough to think the date was going pretty good.

"This can't be the last picture of me," I say.

Louise smiles weakly. "For memory lane, we don't include anybody's death or the direct circumstances that led to it. This is your last photo."

I am dreaming. That's what's happening. And once I wake up I will be alive again and I may not even remember this dream. While I stare at my last "photo," I don't really feel any powerful emotions. So much about it seems arbitrary. My clothes. My hair. My expression. There is no way

I would be smiling if this was really my last photo. *Dream. Dream. Dream.*

"You've got some momentum going. Let's keep moving forward," Louise says.

I do not feel any momentum. This is the saddest dream I've ever dreamt. And what if it's somehow true? What if I did die in the ambulance? That's unimaginable. There is no way I am a dead person. Right?

"When do I get to see my family again?" I ask. "What about my friends?"

"These are all perfectly normal questions and feelings. But what's important right now is to go to the viewing room. Every soul needs to see how they die. Frame by frame. Yours is ready."

"Will I ever see these pictures again?" I ask. It feels wrong to leave them.

"You have completed your walk down memory lane."

But that's not really an answer to my question. "How much longer do they get to stay here?" I ask. "Can I look at them again later?"

Louise shakes her head. "It's completed. It doesn't stay. You don't get another turn."

I look back at the photos and shake my head. I can see that the ones farthest away are beginning to fade and disappear. "You're taking everything from me at once. It's not fair."

She doesn't say anything immediately. And when she finally does speak, her voice is a mixture of calm and sympathy, as if she's applied her most soothing tone. "I'm not doing anything. This is the process."

I find this totally unacceptable. "I hate the process." I want to wake up.

Louise opens a door and lifts her arm like she wants me to enter. "The tough thing about death is that everything that happens now is nonnegotiable. You have to accept what's dealt to you."

"That's utterly heartbreaking," I say as I stare back at my photos and see that nearly half of them are gone.

"Let's keep moving. You need to prepare for your funeral."

"My funeral?" I can't even wrap my brain around that idea.

"It's time," Louise says. The soothing voice now adjusted to communicate a much more forceful tone.

And so it's really going to happen. I am going to watch myself die. I don't resist entering the viewing room with Louise. This moment feels inevitable. This is going to happen whether I like it or not.

eleven

According to Louise, the five stages of grief and the five stages of crossing over are somewhat similar. The first stage is denial. That's where I am.

It's one thing for me to say, *I am Molly Weller and I am dead*. But it's quite another thing for me actually to feel that way.

"I just can't believe that my head injury was fatal," I tell Louise.

What I'm witnessing doesn't feel like a dream anymore. We're watching the final moments of my life on a large white screen. The picture is perfect. And as surprising as it sounds, I'm actually a little eager to watch my own death now. To see how something so bad could have happened to me.

"Oh, that's not what killed you."

"What killed me?" I turn to look at her.

"It's coming up. Watch the bottom left corner."

I turn back to view the last moments of my life. Peppa meanders through the brush. Tate and Salt aren't in the picture. It's just me and my lovely, flatulent, sidetracked horse.

"Look," Louise says, pointing to a large rock.

"That's where I hit my head," I say.

I watch the stupid rock and notice something curled up in a patch of sunlight next to it. It's a snake.

"It's a prairie rattler," Louise says. "Very common for that area, and very aggressive."

Peppa notices the snake and tries to backtrack. Then, terrified, he bucks, tossing me overboard. As I drop to the ground, the butt-first trajectory of my body is aimed right at the snake. That's when I see the snake strike. It happens so fast. The snake flies at me and sinks its fangs into my right buttock. I shouldn't have worn such thin cotton pants. Then I hit my head and am knocked unconscious. I watch as Tate races to me. He leaps off his horse and doesn't see the snake. He takes off his jacket and shirt. Then, using his shirt, he tries to stop the loss of blood from my head. He almost forgets to put his jacket back on.

"He really tried," Louise says.

Tate grabs Peppa's reins and tethers them to a bush.

"Why take the time to do that?" I ask.

"He was afraid that Peppa would wander over and bite you."

"A horse?" I ask.

Louise nods. "Sometimes they do that. Peppa would have tried to rouse you."

I look back to the screen, and I crumble in sadness.

"I don't want to watch any more of this," I say.

"You should. It will help you form your last words."

"I'm already dead."

"Well, that's true, but I have good news. According to some requests you made in the preexistence, you are allowed to speak last words." Louise's tone of voice sounds cheerful, and she continues to explain things to me in a matter-of-fact way. "We'll reinsert you into your body at the moment before you die. Technically, you haven't officially expired on earth, because you haven't released your last breath or said your last words. We collected your soul right before you died, and time is suspended while you're here."

As I absorb the news, it occurs to me that my current situation isn't as bad as I thought. "Well, in that case, stick me back in my body and let me live."

"Molly, it doesn't work that way. It was your time."

No. Did we both just watch the same home movie? "That was a fluke," I say, gesturing with both hands at the screen. "A snake bit me on the butt and everybody was distracted by my bleeding head. What are the odds of that happening? One in three billion? It wasn't my time."

"You had other exit dates."

"I don't believe you," I say. I know she's wrong. This was the only time in my life I'd ever gone horseback riding. "I am never in the wilderness. I bet I could live sixty more years and never see another snake."

"You're misunderstanding. On October twelfth, you would have drowned in Rigby Lake."

I cannot accept my death. I won't. "That's impossible. I don't even swim."

"I think that was the point. You went with Ruthann and Joy and you hit your head and fell into a shallow part and drowned."

"Another head injury?" I ask.

"Not really. It knocks you off balance, and then you drown."

"With Ruthann and Joy?"

"They've already left by the time you're drowning."

"We're not even friends anymore. I was considering quitting the squad," I say. "Just this morning, my cat attacked Ruthann. It was a huge blowup! No way I'd go to a lake with her. I think you've been misinformed."

She sighs heavily at this challenge. "You reconciled with them. October twelfth was a celebration of your renewed friendship."

"Are you sure?" I ask.

I can't believe that I would have let myself be talked into enduring another round with Ruthann. And after she threatened to euthanize Hopkins? I had more love for my cat and more self-respect than that. Didn't I?

"Yes. I'm sure."

"So, we became friends again, and then my friends didn't save me?" Even though this alternate death scene didn't happen, it's still hard to swallow.

"They'd already left. You'd had a fight and you'd all driven there separately. Next. On October twentieth, while trying to avoid a cow in the road, you drove your car into a telephone pole."

"I died in a car crash? For a teenager, that's so cliché."

"Actually, the crash didn't kill you. You were electrocuted by dangling wires while attempting to exit your vehicle. And on October twenty-fourth, you were struck by lightning while seated in the school bleachers during a bomb threat."

"Wow. Would the school have been liable for that?"

"Yes, in this instance, your father brought a lawsuit against the school. Oh, this is terrible."

"What?"

"Basically he surrenders his entire life to avenge your death and never lives another happy day on earth."

"But that doesn't happen, right? Because of the snake death?"

"Yes, you're absolutely right."

I'm too sad to ask what the future of my parents will be without me. And when I think about Hopkins, it just makes me feel worse.

"So, it was my time?" I ask. "From the day I was born, I wasn't meant to turn seventeen?"

"That's correct. I'm so sorry. You died on Saturday, October fifth, at two thirteen p.m."

I know this counselor says that she's sorry, and she sounds sorry, but I don't think she really understands how truly devastated I am. Even though I'm stuck in both denial and shock, I understand that it's October fifth and I am dead. And it's terrible to know this. Because my life was bursting with unaccomplished goals and plans. All I can focus on are the things on my calendar that I was planning to do. My first performance with the Tigerettes. Asking

Tate to the Sweetheart Ball. Going to the Sweetheart Ball. Making up with Sadie. Squaring things away with Henry.

"I was in the middle of everything," I try to explain. "I was just starting to figure things out."

"Everybody feels that way," Louise says. "Even the ninety-year-olds. Okay. Now, you're going to be placed back into your body for the sake of saying last words."

I have no desire to say my last words. What do they matter? "It's just the paramedic. He's not going to care about my last words."

"Molly, it's not just any paramedic. You've got Rustin Pinch. He's a superb soul and will transmit your last words to your parents verbatim. You are very lucky."

Louise is so passionate when she says this, that for a moment I do feel a little lucky. Until I remember that I'm dead. From a fatal snakebite to my butt.

"Louise, can I ask you something?"

"About your parents?"

"How did you know?" I ask.

"Oh, I'm connected to you now. I can't read your exact thoughts, but anything you think in the form of a question gets sent to me. That's my job. I answer your questions."

Whoa. I am not comfortable with that. Nobody should have access to my mind. It's *mine*. But I make a note to myself that my thoughts are hijackable in question form.

I stare at Louise. She stares back.

"Okay. I have a big question. It's about the baby," I say.

"I'm not really permitted to dispense that kind of information."

This afterlife stuff is a little confusing. First, she's here to answer my questions and guide me through the next phase of my existence. Then, she can't divulge the things that I really need to know. I ask my question anyway.

"Is the baby here? In this crossing-over place?"

"No, prebirth, everybody remains in the preexistence. No, Molly, there's no chance you could meet."

Because I hadn't been enthusiastic about the pregnancy, my parents hadn't told me much about the baby. We didn't talk about possible names. I didn't help turn our exercise room into a nursery. When it came time to paint the room buttercream yellow, I attended a Tigerette training camp instead of helping my Aunt Claire. I never got invested. The day they learned the baby's sex, I told them that I didn't want to know. I wanted it to be a surprise. In retrospect, I was being a little passive-aggressive. But now I want to know. Now I wish I'd handled all that differently.

"Is it a girl?"

Louise smiles.

I look down. "I think my mom was hoping to have a boy."

"Well, then, she'll be thrilled."

This makes no sense to me. Louise beams like a person unable to share exceptionally good news.

"She's having twins? My mother is having twins." It seems impossible.

"I can't dispense information."

She winks at me, and I realize that I'm right. My mother is pregnant with twins. Why wouldn't my parents have told me that?

"This feels so weird, Louise."

"Don't focus on that now. Think about your last words."

I close my eyes. Nothing I could say seems profound enough. I should have studied famous quotes or something. Don't dying people usually say remarkable things?

"I think I've got something," I say. "But—"

"Great!" Louise lifts her hands up and rushes toward me like she's going to tackle me. It freaks me out. Is she going to knock me over? Then I feel her energy hit me.

"You're going back. Now, be careful. Don't say anything confusing. You want to leave everyone with a sense of peace."

A flood of energy washes over me, and I realize that I'm dropping back to earth. To Wyoming. To the ambulance. To my body.

As I'm going, a brilliant idea strikes me. It's like after I died I became a genius. Here's my plan. What if I tell Rustin Pinch to look at my butt so he can discover the snakebite and deliver antivenom to me? Couldn't I save my life? As I tumble down to earth, I'm so proud of myself.

"Molly, you can't save your life. They'll discover the bite soon enough. The venom has been coursing through your small body for almost two hours."

No. No. Did I construct my salvation plan in the form of a question? And by doing so, did I just alert my intake counselor to this plan and thereby blow my last shot at life?

"It's your time." Louise's voice echoes around me.

"No. I need a few more minutes."

But it's too late. I can see. And smell. And taste. And hear. I'm back inside the ambulance again. My soul has been rehoused in my wounded body. I can feel the deep gash in my head and the swollen tissue around my butt. Like steady drumbeats, they throb with pain.

"Does your girlfriend have any preexisting medical conditions?" the paramedic yells.

He sounds so worried.

"I don't think so," Tate shouts. "She might be recovering from the flu."

Last words. I need to say my last words. What I say next has the chance to put my parents at peace.

"Molly, I need you to be a good girl and stay awake for me."

I feel him lightly slap my cheeks. It helps bring me around.

"Molly! Be good. Stay with me."

It's time. I have the words.

"Mom." My voice cracks. Is this really happening? I start again. I have to get this right. "Mom, Dad, I love you. Enjoy the twins." I can hardly breathe. But I'm not done. I try to stay focused. I don't want my parents to feel any guilt. "This wasn't anybody's fault."

Rustin tries to argue with me. But it's too late. I let out a long breath and I go with it. Up. Up. Up. It's happened. I am dead. No more life. No more body. I suspect that I'm returning to be with Louise. To her office with the clocks. And the hallway with the photos. I am moving on to the next phase of my existence. Except I have no idea what that actually is.

twelve

When I meet up with Louise again, we're back in her messy office, and I feel like a mess too. Emotionally speaking, death isn't tidy. It's disorienting. I don't know whether I should stand or sit or float. All the clocks on the wall continue to tick. Before I left to say my last words, the sound was faint, but now the ticking is louder; it's counting something down.

"Nice choice of last words," Louise says. "Considering your circumstances, I wasn't expecting you to do this well."

It's unsettling to hear her assume that I would do poorly. "That's not a particularly nice thing to tell a newly dead person."

"It's just that after following you for the last six months, I wasn't sure you'd arrive with enough intention. Or direction."

The idea that a spirit person has been tracking me through my summer vacation and junior year of high school is beyond creepy.

"You seem to be missing that my life was actually going really well," I say. I don't know what Louise thinks she saw, but clearly she didn't catch everything. "I was making a lot of positive changes."

"Befriending Ruthann Culpepper? Pushing away Henry Shaw?"

Louise's judgmental comments make me feel incredibly defensive. No person is perfect. Does she think she's perfect? Maybe dead people *are* perfect. I have no idea. "If I'd known that I was going to die, I would've handled a lot of things differently these last few months," I say, trying to explain myself.

Louise sighs. "I hear that all the time."

Her response makes me feel even more defensive. "Listen. I was backtracking like mad on the Ruthann Culpepper friendship. And I did *not* push Henry Shaw away. He had a girlfriend, Louise. A *serious* girlfriend. Her name was Melka."

Louise looks unconvinced. She doesn't respond right away, and we just sort of stare at each other while the clocks tick. Annoyingly loud.

"So what do they mean?" I ask. "What happens now? What am I supposed to do next?"

Louise looks away and then rolls her eyes.

How rotten. *The intake counselor for my soul is rolling her eyes at me.*

"I think I need to show you something," she says.

Thus far, everything Louise has shown me has been death-related and overwhelmingly depressing.

"You don't have a lot of time before your funeral. You really shouldn't resist," Louise says.

The words echo through me. *My. Funeral.* They should not exist in the same sentence. Not for another eighty years.

"Ready?" Louise asks.

I consider telling her no, or demanding that she tell me more before she takes me somewhere else. But I don't. Now that I'm dead, Louise is the only person I have. I should attempt to stay on her good side for as long as possible.

"Ready," I say. As soon as my consent is spoken, Louise pulls me into a tunnel, and moments later, a wall of green slams into me. It's a pasture. I'm on a farm.

Daylight shines so powerfully overhead that I wonder if she's taken me to a place that's actually closer to the sun. Then I hear the sound of bleating goats and mooing cows and clucking chickens.

Rather than try to guess our location, I ask. "Where are we?"

"A farm," Louise says.

I'm dead. On a farm. With my soul's intake counselor. On a blazingly bright day. My life feels like a puzzle and none of the pieces quite fit.

"Are my parents here?" I don't know why they'd be on a farm. Especially after learning about my death.

"This way," Louise says.

I follow her across a dirt path to a shed surrounded by chickens. Dozens of light brown hens cluck and strut behind a fence of small wire hexagons. Louise enters the coop, and I follow.

"And this chicken coop is relevant to my funeral in *what* way?" I ask.

Louise points to a brown egg resting in a straw-lined box. I notice a small hole on the egg's side. A tiny beak flashes through it, and the egg rolls over, blocking the opening.

"If I was alive, I'd help it," I say.

"And then you'd doom it," Louise says.

The chick redistributes its weight inside the egg, making it roll again, uncovering its already pecked-open area. The beak continues to break out, further enlarging the hole.

"Hatching requires a tremendous amount of effort. The act of breaking out of the shell strengthens the chick's heart and lungs. If you remove the challenge and help the chick, it emerges into life undeveloped and too weak to survive."

"That's a tough way to start life," I say.

While alive, I don't think I ever saw a live flesh-and-feather chicken. I only encountered them in nugget or taco form. Seeing them now feels odd. Are there chickens in the afterlife?

"This is symbolic, Molly," Louise says. "Do you understand what I'm saying?"

Not really. I try to distill it into something somewhat logical. "Death is like an eggshell? And I have to peck my way out?"

"This isn't going to translate exactly," Louise says. "Don't think so literally."

In the time since we've started talking, the chick has made a hole the size of a nickel. It can almost fit its head through.

"Death is like a figurative eggshell?" I ask. How does this symbolism even work? Eggs hatch to start life. Death is the end of life. There's no similarity whatsoever.

"First, Molly, you should understand that this is a period of great freedom for you. You're liberated from your body and all that pain."

Maybe this chicken coop speech would make sense for somebody who died of a slow-progressing cancer or some other long, lingering illness, but not for me. The clucking has grown so loud that it's scattering my attention. I have to will myself to focus on Louise. "Up until the end, I was never in that much pain. And I liked having a body." Louise's words feel like propaganda. I'm *free*? I'm *liberated*? No. I'm *dead*.

"This is your chance to visit the people who love you and help lessen their grief," Louise explains. "The presence of your soul can comfort them."

I've already tired of the coop and am ready to move on. "Okay. I absolutely want to see my family. Tell me how to do that."

"This is where death is like the eggshell," Louise explains.

"You're losing me," I say.

"I'm not going to break open your shell and pull you into this world. That's your job. You emerge on your own. I just give some helpful guidance."

"Okay," I say, hoping that it will suddenly just occur to me how to find my family. "So I locate my loved ones and help them grieve. And is this when I'm supposed to make myself known to them by showing them signs? Maybe I fog a mirror or change a radio station or steer a dove into their path?"

Louise tries to interrupt me, but I don't let her. If she thinks I have to emerge from my shell on my own, I'll show her that I'm actually capable of doing this.

"I've seen shows about paranormal 'hot spots.' I just need to figure out where those are. Once, I saw a show that documented a kitchen hot spot, and when you placed a person on the floor at one end of the kitchen, a spirit dragged them to the other end. In the show I saw, the homeowners actually did this so much with their toddler that it wore their linoleum down to the wooden subfloor."

My mind races with possibilities of how I can communicate with everyone I love. Just because I died doesn't mean that I need to be severed from them. We can still connect. It's just going to be weird and one-sided. Until they die too. And join me. Wait! I wonder if Louise can tell me when everybody I love is scheduled to die. Maybe that's what the clocks mean.

Louise shakes her head. "You don't really have the ability to manipulate matter after you die. You are a soul and you will remain a soul from this point forward."

The chick has now completely hatched from the egg. Its feathers look wet and unfluffy, and its head is too heavy for its slender neck. The bird tries to keep its balance by jerking open its wings, but the chick is so young that it trembles from its newness and just keeps falling down. It looks so weak it seems doubtful that it can survive. This was a terrible object lesson for crossing over. I am nothing like a feeble chick. Nothing.

"What about other souls who love me?" I ask. "Why aren't they here?" It's just starting to come to me that I haven't encountered any dead relatives. "Aren't I supposed to have a spirit guide? What about my grandpa?" I never met him—he died before I was born—but I've seen pictures of him. It seems like a relative should be helping me.

"That's not really how things work," Louise says apologetically. "What you may have heard about death during life is often wrong."

I hope Louise eventually tells me something both useful and positive. "Will I see the white light?"

People talk about seeing a white light when they die, but I feel more like I've entered a tunnel of blackness, with no light in sight.

"This is what I can tell you. You cross over during your funeral. At that time, you move to the next phase."

"So I'm not in the next phase yet?" I'm confused. I thought the next phase was what followed death. But now I'm learning that the next phase follows the funeral. Louise is not a very communicative spirit guide. She should have made this clear from the onset. "What's *this* called?" I ask.

"You are in the process of crossing over. The actual crossing takes place at your funeral."

I steal one last look at the stumbling chick. My ultimate destination. Louise knows what it is, but she's not telling me. How can it be ethical to withhold this from me? It's not, I conclude. I have an unethical intake counselor. Unbelievable. Maybe I can persuade her. Because I have to know my fate.

"Oh, Louise. Where will I go? Heaven? Hell?" I ask. "Please tell me."

As I wait for her answer, a mixture of dread and fear and regret crawls through me. I suspect that her reluctance to fully disclose my fate might be related to the fact that I've inadvertently damned myself. Maybe it's because I wasn't nice enough to people. Maybe it's because I stole things. There are a considerable amount of misdeeds I could have committed that put my postdead fate in jeopardy. And who wants to level a newly dead girl's spirits by telling her that she's going straight to Hell?

"I can't tell you that. You need to focus on crossing over, not about what happens after that."

"I need more guidance," I argue.

"Start your journey by visiting your parents."

Louise doesn't understand what it feels like to die. I can't imagine that watching my parents sob over my fatal accident will nourish me. But I feel ready to go and do something other than stand in a barn feeling terrible and lost.

"If I focus on them, will that show me where they are?" I ask.

"Follow your intuition," she says.

"But I don't feel anything," I say. And isn't intuition what led me to accept a date with Tate, which ultimately caused my death to begin with? Doesn't that mean that I have deadly intuition? That sounds like something I shouldn't be following anymore.

"You should feel something," Louise says.

I shake my head.

"Your parents might not know about your death yet," Louise explains.

The thought of my parents' finding out about my death is too sad for me to entertain for more than a few seconds. "This is awful."

"It gets better."

What is she talking about?

Then it happens. I feel something. It's like I'm being grabbed—violently. "Something is happening," I say.

"Great!" Louise says, returning to her more upbeat demeanor. "Your parents need you."

"But it's going to be so hard to see them again." Panic snakes through me.

"When you come back, we can discuss your three visitations," Louise says.

I don't have time to ask her what that even means. We're not in the same room anymore. I am racing through a tunnel, where everything is gray. Nobody else is here. Where are my parents? Maybe it's just one of them. Maybe they weren't together when they found out. In an instant, the tunnel ends and I am in the world again. *Racing. Racing.* There is sunshine and blue sky. Whatever was pulling me has stopped, and I am in a cluster of pine trees, on a patch of bare earth beside a mountain road. I don't think I've ever been here before. I stand perfectly still as a car approaches. Everything about it looks familiar.

thirteen

It's 8:13 p.m. I died six hours ago, at 2:13 p.m. My parents are driving back from the hospital in Wyoming. Really, I think somebody besides my father should be driving. He's leaning on the steering wheel like he's cradling it for comfort. My mother has her eyes closed. They both look exhausted. I sit in the backseat. There are long moments of silence, and then my mother cries. She tries to muffle her sobs with her hands. When this doesn't work, she buries her face in the sleeve of her jacket. My father leans further into the steering wheel.

"A snake," he says. "A goddamned snake."

When my father mentions the word snake, my mother's crying intensifies. She releases sounds that remind me of a wounded animal. I put my hand on her shoulder, but she doesn't seem to notice.

"We need to read it," my father says.

I see a folded piece of paper in my mother's hand.

"I can't," she says. She doesn't lift her face from her sleeve. Her voice sounds soft and broken.

"But they were her last words."

My mother raises her head. Her eyes are rimmed with a redness in a way I've never seen before. It's otherworldly. She is in such anguish that her pain extends itself to me and I can barely stay near her. "It didn't look like Molly. Beneath that sheet. That tube in her mouth." She buries her head in her sleeve again. "She was so pale."

"They should have taken out the tube before they showed her to us," my father says. "We shouldn't have seen her like that."

I'm not giving them enough comfort. Should I be trying to do something more? Fog the rearview mirror and write my name? Break something? As I ride along, it feels like nobody will be happy ever again. I'm failing.

"I'm going to pull over and we're going to read the note," my father says. He flips on the turn signal and slows down the car.

"No," my mother says. "It's too much."

But my father steers over to a graveled shoulder anyway and shuts off the car. They are more than an hour away from home.

"We're her parents. It's our job to read it," my father says, pulling the paper from her fingers.

My mother isn't objecting anymore. "I wonder if she asked for me. Sometimes children ask for their mothers."

I feel bad. I don't want to disappoint her with my last words, but it never even crossed my mind to ask for her. I was conscious enough to realize that that would have been an absurd request.

"Ready?" he asks.

"I'm never going to be ready."

My father unfolds Rustin's note like it's a precious historical document prone to disintegrate if mishandled. Using one hand, he wipes tears away from his eyes; using the other, he tries to keep the paper steady. He can't. He trembles as he reads aloud from it.

"'My name is Rustin Pinch. I have been a paramedic for six years. I was with Molly when she went into cardiac arrest in the ambulance. I have been with many people when they pass. Sometimes, not always, I think they know what's coming. I think Molly knew. She wasn't in any pain. She went quickly. I'm very sorry for your loss. I hope you find comfort in knowing that you were both very much in her final thoughts. These were Molly's last words.

"'*Mom, Dad, I love you. Enjoy the twins. This wasn't anybody's fault.*'"

My mother begins crying again. I know that no matter what I said, this would have been her reaction. After a minute of steady sobs, she blows her nose and asks, "When did you tell her about the twins?"

"I never told her," my dad says. "Maybe you mentioned them."

"No. I was very careful. My pregnancy was hard on her. She didn't want to hear about it. And I respected that."

"Maybe she meant other twins," my dad says.

"Do we know any twins?" she asks.

"Is one of her friends a twin? Is Joy a twin?"

"No."

"Wait, Tommy Tarry is a twin," he says.

"Who's that?" my mother asks.

"He works at the Thirsty Truck. He has a twin brother named Abe. Molly worked with Tommy a lot last summer."

"Why would she tell us to enjoy them?"

"I don't know. I've been thinking about hiring Abe."

My mother sniffles and shakes her head. Clearly, their grief has disoriented them. *Our twins.*

"Stan, I doubt our dying daughter was concerned about staffing the second shift at the Thirsty Truck. She must've heard us talking." My mother rubs her belly.

"I'm so sorry that you're this sad," I say. "I'm sad too. So sad."

I wonder how long I get to stay. Seeing the house and Hopkins again is going to destroy me. My father starts the car. I am so worried about him driving.

"We need to get home," he says.

And just as I start to calm down and prepare for the long, depressing journey home, I feel the odd sensation of being pulled somewhere by somebody.

"No," I say. I want to stay with my parents.

But the feeling doesn't go away. It gets stronger and stronger. If I wanted to fight it, I could. But I'm curious. The person pulling me is just as sad as my parents are. Is it my grandmother? I look at my parents again. I'll be able to visit them more, right? And they have each other. But the person who is pulling me is all alone. I feel like I should leave. Visit. Provide comfort.

So I release myself from my parents' car and am sucked

into the air, high over the mountains and clouds, moving as fast as when I reentered my life through the gray tunnel. I am zooming over houses and rivers and fields. Then I see a neighborhood. It's not mine, but it looks familiar. Before I can identify where I am, I'm thrown inside a kitchen window, dragged up a short set of stairs, and placed in a dark room. The grief I'm confronting is debilitating. But I don't think it's my grandmother's place. This isn't her house. I see a bed. A desk. A person. Who is that? Oh my god. I know exactly where I am. But out of all the places to be taken second, I can't believe that I wound up here.

fourteen

I am standing next to Henry Shaw. He's curled up on his bed. Soft music flows out of his speakers. It sounds like jazz, but I have no idea who is playing. If I were alive, I could ask him. If I were alive, I could say something funny and cheer him up. If I were alive, Henry wouldn't be sad in the first place.

I'm surprised that his grief would be strong enough to pull me to him. When I died, I wasn't thinking about him at all. Only my parents crossed my mind. I lean down and whisper his name. "Henry?" Because of the Melka situation, because of how things ended between us, I never expected to return to his bedroom. Ever.

"Henry?" I repeat. Even though I know he can't hear me, I feel a strong urge to say his name. And when I do, it makes me feel more connected to him. I move onto the bed. Louise told me that my presence can ease a person's sadness. I press my soul around Henry's body. Can he feel that I'm here? I stay very quiet, very still, as I watch him breathing. My parents didn't seem as affected by my presence, but for

136

Henry my arrival seems to stir something in him. He turns around and faces in the opposite direction; he faces me.

"I can't believe you're dead. How could you die like that?"

I watch him cry. His eyes are swollen and his face is red with sadness. He's looking right at me, but he doesn't know it.

"You were right here. A few days ago. In this room. And you go on one date with Tate Arnold and you wind up dead? Jesus. Why did you even go out with that guy? He's a stupid jock, Molly. He could never appreciate you. He had no idea how funny you are." He starts crying again. "How funny you *were*." His voice gets louder. "This wasn't supposed to happen!"

Henry is breaking my heart. I felt bad enough about being dead before I got here. But seeing this makes me feel sad in a different way. I'm beginning to understand that I didn't just lose what I had, but I also lost what could have happened. My future. All the paths that were ahead of me. They are as dead as I am.

Out of an impulse to comfort him, I start saying anything that comes to mind. "You're going to be fine. You have a long life. I can see it." I have no idea how long Henry Shaw will live. "You'll fall in love. Get married. Have babies. Lots of babies. And there's a ton of jazz." I'm struggling for ideas. "You will become so famous that you will travel by private jet."

Do saxophone players ever get famous? I'm not sure. All I know is that my words do nothing to comfort him. I can feel his sadness, and it's as deep as my parents'. This confuses me. He picked another girl over me. How much could he really have cared about me?

I stare at him on his bed, stuck in grief. I can't take much more of this.

"I didn't want to die, especially not the way I did die, but this was supposed to happen." And I don't say it in a wimpy voice. I say it with total certainty. Because it's not good for Henry to feel this way. And it's not good for me to feel this way either.

He sits up. "I think I'm going crazy. I think I can almost hear you."

"Really?" I ask. "Henry. You are not going crazy. It's me. Molly Weller. I am on your bed. I am helping you grieve."

I see goose pimples form on his skin. He's very sensitive to my soul.

"Molly, if you're here, please give me a sign." His eyes dart around every corner of the room.

A sign? I try to explain. "I can't give you a sign. My spirit guide says that souls don't really do that. Just tune in to what I'm saying, okay?"

"Now it feels like you're gone," Henry says. "Did you leave?"

This is exhausting. I'm expending way more energy here than I did with my parents. It's to the point where I feel flimsy and barely present. "I am right here!" I yell. When I raise my voice, it seems to impact him more.

"Molly, I need to tell you something. Are you still here?"

It's like I'm in a movie, right at the moment where I'm

poised to hear either a crushing confession or something transformative and wonderful. *Don't crush me, Henry.* I should leave. If I don't hear what he says, it will be like he never said it. Sadly, I can't manage to do this, because even dead I am voraciously curious.

"Molly," he whispers.

"I am still here!" I say again. "I am on your bed with you!"

But he doesn't tell me yet. He grabs some Kleenex from a box beside his bed and blows his nose.

"This isn't how I wanted to tell you," he says.

"Say it," I plead. I don't know how much longer I'll be able to stay with him before I get dragged away by a third requester. I mean, my grandma is going to be pulling my soul toward her grief any second. And I'm not going to deny my grandma comfort.

Henry finally speaks. "Molly, I feel like something was supposed to happen with us," he says. "It feels wrong that you died. Are you there?"

This time, I don't answer him. As he speaks these words I let them settle inside me; I believe them. He's right. Something was supposed to happen. His grief mixes with mine, and it hurts me in a way that causes actual pain throughout my soul. "Stop." Maybe if he stops feeling this way, I'll stop feeling this way. But he doesn't. He gets up and walks across the room and turns up the volume on the music. The band plaques on his walls vibrate as a saxophone wails. I keep thinking he's going to pick up his own saxophone and play it and release some of his sadness. But he doesn't.

He sits down at his desk and stares out the window. It's dark outside. Watching him as he zones out into the nothingness of the evening, it's so easy for my mind to cycle back to the last time I was in his room. Kissing Henry felt absolutely right.

"You're going to be okay," I say. In a weird way, it's flattering to see Henry this sad.

Knock. Knock. Knock.

"Henry," a soft voice calls. "It's me. Melka. I heard the news. Can I come in?"

I can't believe it. Ruthann was right. Melka must be a total stalker, because how else did she know to show up at this exact moment? It can't be a coincidence that minutes after Henry's grief summoned me, she's banging on his bedroom door. And I also can't believe that she's referring to my death as "the news." It makes me sound like a headline in a newspaper. I was a person. Melka should say my name. My death is not *the news*. Henry lets her inside his room, and they hug.

"Dis is so unbelievable," Melka says. "I'm sorry. I know you liked Molly so much. She was so funny. So easy to like."

I have two thoughts on this.

First, *Wow.* Weird that his girlfriend would talk about the fact that he liked me *and* build me up. Is this some sort of relationship-saving reverse-psychology strategy that people use in Eastern European countries? I would be furious if I knew that my boyfriend liked another girl. And if that girl died, I would feel terrible, but I wouldn't focus on how likable and funny she was. Would I?

Second, I'm glad she called me by my name.

"You seem surprised by his sadness," a voice says. Freaked out that somebody is standing next to me, I whirl and scream. It's Louise.

"What arc you doing here?" I ask. She shouldn't invade Henry's bedroom like this.

"I told you I'd be here for your entire journey."

"Everything about this sucks," I say. "Everything."

"Are you just beginning to understand how much hc liked you?" Louise asks.

"Don't you get it, Louise? He chose Melka over me. He's with her right now. See?"

I dramatically swing my arm out toward Melka and Henry. But they aren't locked in some supportive embrace or holding hands or anything. They're just sitting on the floor together. Looking at something. Whoa. It's a picture of me.

"I don't understand how that relationship works at all," I say.

"Gricving is a very draining process," Louise says. "Henry needs company."

"Why do you keep downplaying the fact that Melka is his girlfriend?" I ask.

"Like I said, I've been following your life with great focus for six months. Henry and Melka broke up."

"And got back together," I say.

"Well," Louise counters, "that's complicated."

I am so sick of hearing that phrase. "Okay," I say. "Right. Do you want to know what's complicated? My death!

That's complicated." I leave Henry's room, burst through three walls, and enter the Shaws' backyard. I'm furious, and as I pass the side of the house, a motion detector light goes off and floods the sidewalk with a pale yellow glow. It startles me that I can make this happen. I catch a glimpse of Louise, and she seems surprised too.

I wish I could smell the grass. Or trees. Or night air. Until you lose your body, you don't understand how much it gave you. I miss it. Trying to comfort myself, I focus on what I can see. Henry's backyard is parklike and adorable. I've never been in it before, but it's a meticulously groomed bed of grass, lined with evergreens on both sides for privacy. It strikes me as the perfect place to picnic, or tan, or make out, or just hang around and relax. They even have a hammock! Louise stands beside me.

"I don't like helping people grieve," I say. "It hurts."

"I know," Louise says.

She doesn't know. "I'm mad. Really mad. I want everything to be different. This is way more final than I thought it would be."

"Anger is part of the grieving process. For you and them."

"Stop talking to me like you're a textbook. This isn't what I need right now."

Louise stands next to me while I pity myself in Henry's backyard. Then I hear voices. Henry and Melka aren't in his bedroom anymore. They've moved to the den, where a window is open. Soon I can hear Melka telling Henry he should play. She tells him several times. Finally he agrees.

And then I can hear Henry's saxophone. For some reason, instead of enjoying the music, listening to it makes me pity myself even more. This time, hearing Henry play means something different to me than it did when I heard him play in his bedroom. This time it means that life will go on for everybody. Except me.

"I should have made different choices," I say.

"Nobody makes perfect choices," Louise says.

I turn to Louise and reach out to her. "I am begging you. Please tell me where I go after I cross over. I need reassurance that I'm not going to be alone. I can't handle it. I need my friends. I need my family. I need to know that I get to be with them again."

Louise looks at me with such concern that a new fear surfaces inside me. I'm not going to see my family and friends ever again. This is it. And she knows it.

"Where you go next depends a lot on the direction you'd already aimed your life."

What? Other than securing a triangle point on the Tigerettes and asking a guy to a girls'-choice dance, my life didn't have much of an aim at all. My anxiety feels like it could clobber me. I look Louise in the eye again and hope she'll understand that I need answers. "Will the people I love come too? Will they follow me?"

"Molly, I can't give you these answers. Your crossing is unique to yourself."

My mind feels empty and crushed.

"A lot of times when people are in their deepest sorrows, they have their clearest insights," Louise says.

I want Louise to stop talking.

"Tell me. Which of your regrets is giving you the greatest discomfort?" Louise asks.

But all my regrets are forming one giant lump of sadness. I can't sort through them.

"I usually counsel people to focus on one act they wish they could undo. And concentrate on it. Then explore how that act put them on a path that helped give their lives their unique shapes. Our actions define us. They shouldn't be regrettable. They created you."

This is the stupidest exercise anybody has ever unleashed into the world.

"During your life, while I followed you, I felt a lot of regret centered around your theft issues."

I cut her off. "I don't want to talk about that."

"You either come to grips with it now, or you store it, let it weigh on you, and carry it longer. You will have to deal with it eventually."

"There's nothing to deal with. I wasn't a perfect person. And I wasn't even thinking about that kind of regret. I was thinking about Henry and my parents and their unending grief," I said.

Louise moves to the center of Henry's lawn, out of the pool of light made by the motion detector. Under the dark sky, on top of the nearly black lawn, she lifts her delicate arms over her head and spins around. "I used to be a dancer."

I have been so busy coming to terms with my own death that I never considered that Louise used to be a person.

But that makes sense. She's a soul. And to end up a soul, you probably had to be a person first. In her pantsuit she doesn't automatically look like a dancer, but watching the outline of her soul move gracefully in circles convinces me that she was.

"I was connected so deeply to my body that when I was separated from it I became obsessed with being near it. That's all I did before I crossed. I didn't help people grieve. And I didn't process what I should have processed."

Watching Louise spin around on the grass and confess her failings convinces me of one thing: I should probably spend less time with her and continue to seek out the people I actually love. She sashays toward me and then away from me, gently covering the distance of Henry's entire backyard. I don't want to do what Louise did. I can't imagine seeking out my body and staying with it like that. My body isn't me. What I am right now. What's left. That's who I am.

As she continues to dance, Louise begins talking to me. "Have you ever asked yourself why you steal? Where all that started?"

Maybe Louise is trying to win some sort of award for being the worst spirit guide ever delivered to a dead person. Thus far, she has made zero effort to try to cheer me up.

"When you dance on the grass and ask me these things, it makes me feel like you don't care about how rotten I feel," I say. I want my spirit guide to be in touch with my misery. And maybe steer me out of it and give me useful postlife advice. Is that so wrong?

Louise stops spinning and returns to my side. "I just

shared something very personal with you. Maybe you should return the gesture."

I am not opening myself up to Louise Davis. "I feel too terrible right now to dig through those issues."

"Dig through them now. Dig through them later. Eventually, you face them."

"I'm done here," I say.

"Are you sure?" she asks.

The sound of Henry's saxophone stops, and I think I can hear Melka laughing. She should be sad like me. And Henry. And everyone else who knew me. Melka shouldn't be laughing.

"Yes. I'm sure," I say.

I still have a lot of people left to visit. If this part of death really is like pecking my way out of an egg, I feel like I've barely cracked the shell.

fifteen

can tell by the brusque way Louise ushers me toward a gray tunnel that she's disappointed in me.

"I'm not going to force you to talk about anything you don't want to talk about," she says.

But that's a manipulative tactic that I've seen used before—by my mother. Doesn't Louise understand that I can see right through her motives? By bringing it up again, she's extending the conversation. And I have no desire to think about why I steal. Why did she have to bring it up? The world around me blurs as I fly through it.

"It's my job to help you cross. And understanding your unhealthy behavior might help you correct it."

At the exact moment we land in her office, I have an obvious realization. I really need to quit thinking in the form of a question or Louise will never stop reading my mind. "Now that I'm dead, I'll probably never steal again. I mean, I can't even pick stuff up anymore."

"Most people spend their whole lives wrestling with

147

something. Crossing over gives them the chance to let those things go."

"Thanks," I say. My mind flashes to Sadie's ring. I should have given that back. Out of all the things I took, that's the item I feel worst about. What will happen to it now? If my mom finds it, she may not know what it is. She might give it away. And it belongs with Sadie.

As I follow Louise out of her office to the hallway, I notice that something awful has happened to the clocks on the wall. Three of them have exploded. Pieces of glass and some sort of metal lie scattered on the floor.

"You've been vandalized," I say. I didn't realize that sort of thing could happen to a spirit adviser.

"No," Louise says. "Don't worry about the clocks. You still have a huge majority left. You're in great shape."

"Why should I care about the clocks?" I say. "Do they come with me?"

I think back to the names of people from my life that are printed on them. Maybe something has happened to them. Maybe three people I love have died! "Did something happen on Earth?" I ask. My mind plays through the worst tragedies. Tornados. Bombs. Nuclear war.

"Other than your death, no grand tragedy has struck your loved ones."

I approach the pieces on the floor and find three names: Deidre Dalton, Sissy Heston, Melka Klima.

"So none of these people are dead?" I ask. Even though I don't know how I did it, I feel somehow responsible for the destruction of Melka's clock.

"They are all alive. Melka, if she stays the course, will become an anesthesiologist."

"What do the clocks mean? Can you tell me that much?" I understand that the clocks are important. But I don't understand why.

"I can say this much. At the time of your death, these clocks represent the most meaningful connections you made while alive. They represent paths and connections still available to you. The more clocks, the more options you have when you pass. You want options. I crossed with about half of my clocks intact. And I was much older, so I had more clocks."

"Is having half your clocks good?" I have other questions I want to ask Louise about the clocks and about her. But I'm not sure if she'll answer any more. She's vague as a counselor. Seriously. What exactly does she mean by "connections" and "paths"? And did she have a family? If so, where are they now? And how old was she when she died? And how exactly did she die?

"With half my clocks left, I was and am able to explore relationships with lots of different people. That's all I can say."

I feel like I'm getting somewhere and nowhere at the same time. It feels good to know there is a system, even if I don't understand how it works. "So, what makes a clock break? What did I do to Deidre?"

"Sometimes it isn't about what you did. Sometimes it's about what they did. But anger often breaks a clock. So don't get angry. That's some advice I can give you."

149

"Thanks," I say. But I'm already getting a little mad that she's not giving me more information. And I'm also not sure how to make myself feel less mad.

"We need to talk about something before you get pulled away by grief again. I'm a little surprised you've gone this long without another tug." Louise says.

"You're right," I say. "Shouldn't more people be grieving for me?"

"Sometimes it takes longer for news of out-of-state deaths to circulate. Don't worry about that. You were loved. And those who loved you will seek you out. I'm certain."

I like hearing that my intake counselor is certain.

"I have great news to give you. In keeping with a request you made in the preexistence, I am happy to inform you that you get to live three life moments over again."

I wish I could remember making these requests.

"What kinds of moments?" I ask.

"Any moments you want," she says.

As I flash through my sixteen years, I'm not sure which moments to choose. Happy ones? That makes the most sense. Then I think of something practical. "You should have told me about this before I walked down memory lane. That way I could have been looking for moments."

Louise nods. "Good point. But memory lane is over."

"Yeah, but in the future. Maybe the next dead girl, you could tell her before." My mind goes back to some of the pictures. It will take me a long time to choose which moments to relive.

"Maybe this will help," Louise says. "You don't have to

recall the exact moment you want to relive. You can simply request to relive your happiest moment. And you'll be transported right to it. All memories are tied to emotions. You're very lucky. Not everybody gets to relive three."

I do not feel lucky.

"And all physical sensation returns when you relive them. You can't change anything, but you'll inhabit your body again. You truly relive the moment."

"Cool," I say. Except that I'm dead. And there's really nothing cool about that.

"You have until your funeral, and it's best not to put those things off," Louise says.

"You just told me about it two minutes ago. You shouldn't rush me. I'm going to really mull this over and choose wisely." Before I died, I never used words like *mull*. My mother used words like *mull*. What's happening to me?

"My best counsel would be to pick moments that help you move forward."

But I don't know if that's what I want. If it's the last time that I'm going to be inside my body, I should probably choose thrilling moments. Times in my life when I felt really powerful things. Before I can mentally sort through some of these, I'm struck by something. Grief! "Oh my god!" I say. "I'm getting pulled." Just like before, it feels intense and awkward. "Do you think it's my parents again?"

"Don't speculate," Louise says. "Just go with it. Somebody who loves you is grieving, and they need you."

Everything is moving too fast. Gray tunnel. Open sky. The suburbs of Idaho Falls. A house. Too fast to tell whose.

I'm drawn through a closed window. I'm standing next to a pool table. Who in my life owns a pool table?

"Joy Lowe!" I say her name as she enters the room. Just like Henry, she looks like she's been crying for hours. I wonder who told her. It's so sweet that she cares about me this much. I walk toward her. "It's okay," I say. I want to provide as much comfort as possible.

"This is still so incredibly unbelievable! It just keeps hitting me over and over," a voice calls from the hallway. "I think I actually need a beer. I think I'm in shock. Do you want one?"

"No," Joy says weakly. "And you shouldn't have one either. My parents count them."

Ruthann enters the room with a silver can in her hand. Her superficial wounds are plastered with Band-Aids and squares of gauze. Hopkins didn't attack her that badly; she's going for sympathy wearing that much bandaging. She flips the tab on her beer and a gasp of air escapes. "But we're grieving."

I cannot believe that I'm visiting Ruthann Culpepper before my grandmother. Something is definitely wrong. Didn't my grandma love me?

"She was acting so weird right before she died," Ruthann says. "It's almost like she knew."

Joy sits down on a big brown couch and shakes her head. "I don't think she knew," she says. "She seemed so happy. Really excited about Tate. Still super into Henry. Her grades weren't as good as they were last year, but she was happy."

Ruthann takes a drink and sits down next to her. "And she had the drill team. It's actually really fortunate for her that she turned her life around in the months before she died and started doing more meaningful stuff."

"I think she was on the brink of making lots of changes," Joy says. "She was going through a growth spurt. I feel so bad that we were in a fight when she died. I wasn't *that* mad at her. I wasn't really mad at all. That night at the mall, everything just came out wrong."

I never knew that Joy cared this much about me. She was a good friend. But we could have been—should have been—closer. That fight was so stupid. And while I'm glad she feels bad about it, I don't want her to feel *this* bad. I sit beside her on the couch. "It's okay. Forget about the fight," I tell her. Joy turns toward me. She is genuinely sad that I'm gone.

"Roy has called me and left three really sweet messages," Joy says. "He's worried about me."

"Ekles?" Ruthann asks.

"Yes. But I don't feel like talking to guys right now. I feel fragile and sad and guilty."

"Death is majorly complicated," Ruthann says.

"I feel like I should call her friend Sadie and talk to her," Joy says. "That friendship was really important to Molly. And they were on the outs. I bet Sadie needs to talk to somebody. I bet she's feeling a lot like I'm feeling."

Ruthann leans forward and sets her beer on the edge of the pool table. Then she eases back onto the couch, nestling her head against Joy's shoulder. "We're all feeling terrible.

But I don't know that we need to hunt down Sadie. She never even liked us."

"She didn't like you because you were a jerk," I say.

"I need to call her," Joy says, standing up.

Ruthann shakes her head. "Not tonight. Let her pull herself together. The last thing she needs it to be blindsided by a late-night phone call she wasn't expecting."

"I guess you're right."

"You know who we should call?" Ruthann says, raising her eyebrows dramatically. "Tate."

Joy sits back down. "No way!"

"I actually called him already, and I'm waiting for him to call me back," Ruthann says. "I know some people might find it awkward to talk to somebody who recently fired them and then witnessed a fatal accident, but I don't feel that way. I feel like talking to him now could really help us reestablish a friendship."

"I bet Tate feels like total shit," Joy says.

I haven't thought that much about Tate. I bet he does feel terrible. I mean, he was with me in the ambulance when I died. He tried to save me. Why hasn't he pulled me to his side? Maybe Louise doesn't totally understand how the rules work. Out of everybody, Tate would be the one who would be reeling from my death with a painful intensity. Why hasn't he wanted me to comfort him? It doesn't make sense. I need more information. I was basically a good person. Shouldn't my postlife experience feel better than this? I feel myself getting angry. Really angry.

"If you could see what's happening to your clocks right now, you'd shudder," a voice says.

I look and see Louise next to me on the couch.

"I'm dead and I'm angry," I say.

"Move toward acceptance," Louise says.

This is ridiculous. She must not normally work with teenagers who die tragically. Acceptance is going to take a while.

"This is very hard for me, Louise," I explain. "Ruthann is awful. She wants to kill my cat. Plus, she's not even properly grieving for me." It disgusts me to admit this, but witnessing Ruthann's reaction to my death hurts me. She isn't genuinely sad.

"I am aware of the emotional limitations of Ruthann Culpepper. But remember, nobody is perfect," Louise says. "For your sake, move past this."

She makes it sound so simple that I get even angrier. "I'm not talking about being perfect. She's really terrible! Look at her over there, decorated in bandages, drinking a beer and using me as an excuse to imbibe it."

"You wasted time in your life with her. Don't waste time in your death. And be nice!"

I get up off the couch. "Fine. I love everybody in this room. I love everybody in the world."

"Maybe you should visit other family members," Louise says.

"They can pull me when they need me," I say.

"You can go find them," Louise says.

"Maybe," I say.

"And there's still that matter of your three life moments," Louise reminds me, following me out the front door of Joy's house. I know I don't need to use doors, but I like behaving the way I did when I had a body. It makes me feel normal.

"I know. I know," I say. "I don't want to choose wrong. I'm still figuring those out."

"Well, then, I'll leave you alone," Louise says.

"Wait! Wait!" I say. "Before you go, could you tell me where to find my grandma?" I'm not sure how to track down people in transit. I doubt my grandmother is at her home in Utah. Am I just supposed to scan the interstate until I feel something?

"Every soul has two instincts. They are centered around your loved ones and your body. During this time, you will always be able to navigate the distance to find your loved ones. And your body."

"My body?" I say. "That sounds so creepy."

"Don't think of it that way. Your body housed your soul for sixteen years. They're connected. They're still naturally drawn to each other."

"I don't want to go looking for my body. I want to find my grandma," I say. I remember the story Louise told me about staying around her body and missing reliving her life moment and not comforting people. What if I became so overwhelmed that I did that too? I don't need to see it. I don't.

"I'm confident you can find her," Louise says.

Fine. I'll do it on my own. I stop thinking about everything and everyone, and focus on my grandma. "She's not with my parents. She's not at her house." I concentrate on her face. Suddenly, I can see her. "I figured it out," I say. "I can see where she is. She's with my aunt Claire. I can really see them, Louise. They're drinking tea in the kitchen. Can you see people like this? Wow. This is so weird. It's like I have superpowers."

"Not quite," Louise says.

I don't hesitate in leaving Ruthann and Joy. They have each other. Though I wish they'd leave Tate alone. He doesn't need to be bothered right now by those two. I shouldn't distract myself. My grandma. Focus. I'm going to see my grandma.

"I need a transport tunnel," I say.

And it's as simple as that. I make the tunnel appear and then I'm in it, surrounded by gray walls, racing toward my grandmother. Soon I see the city. It's late morning and I'm dropping through a pink-lit sky. Falling with tremendous speed.

Slipping through clouds, I grow nervous about what awaits me. When I visited Henry, it was so painful. I hesitate.

And now, in midtumble, when I look around, the neighborhood doesn't seem exactly right. I'm not in Blackfoot. This is Idaho Falls. I glimpse the Snake River. The airport. And then I'm pulled through a red roof. And then I'm underwater. This can't be Aunt Claire's house. There are legs all around me, kicking and thrashing. I let my soul rise to the surface, and I look around. Women decked out in swim caps, wearing leg weights, lift their arms in time to some rock music. I'm in what appears to be a hotel swimming pool that does not contain either my grandmother or my aunt Claire.

My hesitation caused this. I've run off course, and this feels exactly as it should feel: unsettling. I climb out of the water and walk through the hotel lobby. A large chandelier hangs over the registration area. People are checking out. Families. Businessmen. Vacationing couples. Their suitcases depress me. One woman is holding a map, tracing her finger along a river.

"We can rent a canoe here," she tells her boyfriend or husband or fiancé or whatever.

I burst through the hotel's large glass window and stand on the street. I will never stay in a hotel again. Or go on vacation. Or rent a canoe with my boyfriend. Or fiancé. Or husband. I will never attend an aerobics class in an over-chlorinated pool. All of this has been taken from me. I look back into the hotel. I watch as a man pulls a red apple from a fruit bowl and bites into it. And I wonder how long that guy has left. How long do any of them have? They can't all be healthy. Somebody in there must have heart disease. Or cancer. Or something. When I was hit by death, I had no idea it was coming. It was the most unfair way to die. Why couldn't I have been sick? If I'd had time to prepare and wrap things up, I wouldn't feel so cheated. I could have done a few more things. Settled affairs. Finished business.

I'm so jealous at the thought of somebody inside that

hotel dying a slow death from a tumor, constructing a list of last things to do, and checking those items off that list, that I have to turn away. If I had a choice, I would stand here and pity myself for days. I'd pity everything I've lost. But I don't have that kind of time. If I want to see and comfort people before I cross, I've got to do it now. Because if I don't, I may never see them again.

sixteen

The pull to leave the sidewalk is unmistakable. My grandmother's grief is so powerful that it's finally come for me. And I let it take me.

As soon as I surrender, I'm immediately yanked into the street. Something feels unusual and more intense than my other comfort trips. Is my grandma in traffic? I try to picture her and locate her, but it doesn't work. I see myself. But not how I am now, and not how I used to be. I'm in a casket. Oh my god. It's my body. I'm not being pulled by my grandma. I'm being pulled by *it*.

I try to resist going forward, but it doesn't work. I'm being dragged through the street, tugged through a bread truck, and finally jerked through racks of pastries and doughnuts and snack pies. Then I'm on the road again, being pulled with an intensity that I've never experienced before. Through more cars. Over sidewalks. Under bridges. Around trees. How far am I going to have to travel like this? Will my body still be in Wyoming?

It must have just arrived. That must be what's happening.

My body made it to town and it wants to reconnect with my soul. No. I don't want to see myself get made up by the mortuary workers. No. I can fight this. I think of something else. My grandma. For some reason, I can't make myself conjure her up. I think. I think. Nothing happens. Block after block. I'm almost to the old part of town, which houses the two main mortuaries. There is only one thing I can think of that will stop my progress. Even though I don't feel totally prepared to do this, I need to relive a life moment.

My mind races through my childhood and teen years. It saddens me that this doesn't take that long. What should I experience again? Who do I want to see and feel? Everyone. But it was so rare that we were all together. My father worked so much. I'm running out of time. Then I remember that I don't have to pick an exact moment. Instead, I can select a sensation. Luck. I want to feel lucky and be with my family. That's the moment I want to relive. "Luck and happiness and everybody I love in one place!" I yell. "That's the life moment I want to relive right now!"

All movement stops. The traffic-packed roadway disappears, and in front of me I see a carnival. And my family. And I even see myself. I look so young, dressed in a pink sundress. Nobody is moving. I walk into the portrait and approach my frozen self. My face is filled with joy. I am on the verge of tossing a ring onto the neck of a glass milk bottle. I don't hesitate. I let my soul walk into my eight-year-old body, and the scene unfolds.

"Don't expect to win," my dad says. "All these games are rigged."

"There's always a few winners," my mother says, patting me gently on the shoulder.

I can't make myself do anything other than what I actually did eight years ago. But I can feel everything. The air is laced with the smell of buttered popcorn and cotton candy. And my hands feel sticky from a cherry snow cone that I just finished.

"I feel lucky," I say. "This plastic ring will land perfectly on top of that bottle."

I lean forward over the counter.

"Gotta stay behind the line," the carnival worker says.

I shuffle back a step and stand up a little straighter. I glance down at my pink sandals decorated with yellow sunflowers. They were my favorite shoes that summer. The night I got them, I even slept in them.

"She's eight years old," my father argues. "We don't need to nail her to the wall with rules."

"If I let everybody lean, I wouldn't have any stuffed animals left. The challenge is what makes this a real game," the worker says. He claps his hands and cheers me on. But I suspect he wants me to lose.

"Aim short," Sadie coaches. "The last one went past it."

"Right," I say. "I saw that." I extend my arm and practice throwing the plastic ring several times. I know what happens. I know I win my next toss. But my eight-year-old self is overwhelmed by the anticipation and has tons of adrenaline coursing through her system.

"Winning is overrated," my grandma says. "You should be having fun."

"I am going to win," I say. I let the ring fly from my fingertips. It sails less than three feet and catches the edge of a bottle. It circles and circles and finally falls. *Clink!*

"You won!" Sadie cheers, grabbing me from behind. "You get anything you want!"

"Nice job," my grandma says. "With that kind of tactile judgment, you could grow up to be a surgeon."

"No way," I say. "I want to make chocolate art for a living."

My mother laughs. "We watched a show on cable last week, a documentary about a famous chocolate artist. He replicates Renaissance paintings in three-inch-by-three-inch chocolate squares."

"Sounds delicious," my grandma says.

"I want to be your assistant," Sadie says.

"Okay," I say. "But be careful. Tempered chocolate is extremely hot. There's a serious risk of burns."

"I will be so careful," Sadie says.

"All right, Molly," my dad says. "Pick your toy."

"The peacock!" I cry.

Of course I pick the peacock. It's the biggest stuffed animal at the stand.

"Here you go!" the worker says. "And may you stay this lucky forever."

"I will!" I say, galloping off with my prize. The sun pounds down on me, and I skip over the asphalt. The dark surface makes the air above it steam. All my life, heat used to bother me, but feeling it again now, I can't get enough of it. I enjoy the sensation of sunlight warming my exposed shoulders while heat wafts up from below. Sadie catches up to me and grabs my hand.

"You're a winner!" she hollers.

We run ahead of my parents. Ahead of my grandma. I focus on how it feels to run. I focus on the temperature of the air around me. Sadie and I skip and gallop and rush forward toward more adventure. Where do we go next? I don't remember. A small rock slips into my sandal, and the weight of my body lands on it. A piercing pain shoots through my heel, and it's thrilling to feel something so specific. Then the pain starts to dull. My moment is ending. I know I don't get to stay in my body much longer.

There are so many things I wish I'd done. There was grass nearby. Why didn't I slip off my sandals and run through it? And there was a slide just a few feet away. Moreover, I completely bypassed the petting zoo. Why was I in such a hurry? The sound of the carnival hums through me. Roller coasters. Popcorn machines. People laughing. I run alongside Sadie, clutching her sticky hand. My stuffed peacock smells like sawdust. Poorly sewn and overstuffed, my toy will burst within the year, and my mother will throw it away.

I'm still running, but there is no Sadie. No carnival. I'm a soul again. Standing on a street corner where people around me are dressed for fall. Jackets. Scarves. A few of them are already wearing gloves. Is it that cold out already? I can't feel anything. An overly bundled-up woman pushes her baby stroller through me. The morning is ticking away. I shouldn't stand on this corner much longer. If I don't visit somebody soon, my body will try to find me. I'm not ready for that. I'm not ready for that at all.

My grandma? Sadie? Tate?

Things went so disastrously wrong when I tried to visit my grandma that it seems like it might be a mistake to try her next. Maybe she isn't ready for me yet. Maybe that's why I went off course and landed in the pool. She may need more time. I try to relax and figure out where I should go. One name keeps surfacing. *Sadie.* Of course I should visit Sadie. In a way, I was just with her.

I'm traveling faster than ever, speeding through the world with a ferocity that would break a body apart. Then I'm in the sky. Blue everywhere. And I fall into a car. Sadie is driving. The radio is blasting, and she's got on dark sunglasses. Dressed in jeans and a cute green jacket I've never seen before, she looks unlike her normal self. Fashionable.

"Do you even know I'm dead?" I ask.

She doesn't answer me and keeps driving. She flips through her CDs until a song featuring a ukulele pulses out of the speakers. If I were alive and riding in this car with her, I would tease her for listening to this sort of music. Possibly I would turn it off. She cranks it.

"You idiot!" Sadie yells.

A tense anger fills the car. It pushes me away from Sadie. This is a new energy, unlike anything I've felt before.

"Never in a million years would I have thought this could happen to you!" Sadie shouts.

I guess she knows.

"Calm down. Where are you going?" I know we can't have a real conversation, but for some reason I like to pretend that maybe we will.

"Shit!" Sadie yells.

I watch as she swerves to miss a squirrel.

"Don't be afraid to hit a squirrel," I say. "And please stop driving like a crazy person."

Sadie continues to drive at a high rate of speed. "What am I supposed to do?" she asks. "You left a total mess. And who's going to clean it up? Joy Lowe? I doubt it. Ruthann Culpepper? No, Molly. She won't. Because you befriended a ridiculous narcissist." She rips off her sunglasses and tosses them onto the seat. Her eyes are red. She wipes tears away.

"You're being really hard on me," I say. I stare at the sunglasses that have fallen through my lap.

"Did you think I was stupid?" Sadie asks, hitting the steering wheel.

Her energy is so intense and angry that I find myself forced outside the car, sitting on top of the roof. I have to fight against her anger to get back inside and remain next to her.

"Ease up or I can't stay," I explain. "I'm trying to give you comfort. You can't aim all this anger at me."

Sadie inhales three deep breaths. "I know what's in your room."

This is bad. Because I think she means the stuff I've stolen. I had no idea that Sadie knew I took things and kept them in my room.

"You think I don't know that you had a serious impulse-control disorder? You think I didn't notice when things went missing?"

Her energy again tries to drive me away. I focus on the sadness I can feel underneath her anger, and I cling to it and remain beside her.

"I feel terrible about that stuff," I say. "I tried to stop. But sometimes one person can't control everything."

"And what are your parents going to think when they find it? Stealing stuff was so stupid. And so was dying."

Tears run down her cheeks and land on her jeans. She shouldn't be driving. She should be at home. Why are all these grieving people driving?

"I'm right here," I say. "I'm trying to comfort you."

"Jesus," Sadie says. "If we ever meet in the afterworld, the first thing I'm going to do is punch you in the face."

"Okay," I say. It takes every last shred of focus to keep me in the car with her. "It's hard for me too. You think I want to be dead? You think I want my parents to find what I've taken?"

"I feel like I should try to fix things," Sadie says. "And how can I do that? Break into your house? Hire a professional cat burglar?"

She makes everything sound impossible. But I see the reality of what she's saying. "It's not your problem. You don't have to undo what I did."

"This isn't my job! It's who you were. Shouldn't your parents know?"

It's hard for me to imagine my parents finding out that I stole from my friends and family and also perfect strangers. I even stole from the store. They won't understand. My dad will freak out, and my mother will be crushed. I hope they don't overreact and start thinking terrible thoughts like, *We didn't even know our own daughter.* What if finding out damages our connection? If anything happened to their clocks, I don't know what I'd do.

Sadie pulls her car into a driveway, but it's not hers and it's not mine. I feel the urge to stay with her, but I also feel a tug toward the house. I try to figure out which friend Sadie is visiting. Then I realize where I am. I'm at Tate's house! Why did Sadie drive here? Is she even friends with him? I'm confused.

Sadie gets out of her car. And when she does, I tell myself not to follow her. I talk to my soul like it's a dog. "Stay put! Stay put!" Arriving at the doorstep of every grieving person is exhausting.

I am still following Sadie. No. I don't want to be here. "Stay put!" I yell again. And finally my soul slows down. I don't want to see Tate. I don't want to be around angry Sadie. My soul is on the verge of stopping, but then I hear Tate's voice.

"Are you okay?" Sadie asks him.

Why is Sadie even at Tate's?

"No," Tate says. "This is the worst thing that's ever happened to me."

"Me too," Sadie says.

I pass through several walls until I reach Tate's room. It's a mess. There are clothes and sports equipment and books and DVDs scattered all over his floor and desk and bed. Unlike Henry, he doesn't have band plaques on his walls—he's got the standard dude posters: swimsuit centerfolds. Mostly blondes. Where are all the pictures of his trips? Belize, Peru, New Zealand, Costa Rica?

Sadie sits on the messy floor with him. They both look exhausted and, oddly enough, a little panicked.

"I didn't understand your message," Tate says. "You need things from Molly's room?"

"I didn't do a good job explaining it," Sadie says.

"You said Molly was a thief," Tate says. "You called her a maniac."

Oh my god. Sadie is trying to ruin my life. Except I'm dead, so she's trying to ruin people's memories of me.

"You suck, Sadie Dobyns," I say. "I withdraw all comfort from you."

"You're jumping to conclusions," a voice says. I turn and see Louise, standing next to Tate's combination clothes hamper and basketball hoop.

"Please, not now," I tell Louise. "I can't miss any of what Sadie is saying. It's cripplingly devious in ways I can't quite wrap my head around."

"Molly wasn't a maniac thief," Sadie says. "She had a disorder. She was a kleptomaniac. She stole things."

"From you?" Tate asks. He doesn't seem to be judging me. Neither does Sadie. They both seem genuinely concerned.

"Yeah. From me. From stores. From other friends," Sadie explains.

"Was she ever caught?" Tate asks. "Arrested?"

Sadie shakes her head. "She was careful. Nobody knew. Not her parents. Not her friends. Nobody. Except me."

Tate nods. "Weird."

"Even dead, I don't want Tate to think that I'm weird," I tell Louise.

"What does it matter? It's not like he was your soul mate," Louise says.

This startles me a little. "Something could have happened between us. He's a very attractive and well-traveled person."

"I see that you relived one of your life moments," Louise says.

"Shh," I say. "They're talking about me. I need to listen."

"But you've still got—"

"Louise, I'm missing important stuff."

"I think you should—"

"Go away! I know I have things to finish. But this is important too."

"Your grandmo—"

"I know!" I say. "Please go!"

I can feel Louise exit, and I turn all my attention to Sadie and Tate.

"I don't want her parents to find what's in her room," Sadie says. "We need to get it."

"You mean, break into Molly's house?" Tate asks.

"Don't be overly dramatic. All we need to do is get me inside her room for ten minutes. I need a couple of people to help me."

"I can't do this with Ruthann Culpepper." Tate's expression registers total abhorrence.

"We won't do this with Ruthann Culpepper. I've asked Henry Shaw to help."

Tate looks like he's reconsidering.

"What do you need me to do?" he asks.

Sadie smiles for the first time since I found her. "I'll go to her house and get into her room. Henry will wait outside her window. I'll gather everything and give it to him. I need you to come to the door after five minutes. And talk to her mom and keep her occupied so I can be alone in Molly's room."

"I can't have a conversation with Molly's mom," Tate says. "I can't face her right now."

"But you didn't do anything wrong."

"It doesn't feel that way. I took Molly on a date and now she's dead. I can't help you."

"But I need your help."

Tate stands up. He starts crying. "This is too much. Way too much."

Sadie gets up to leave. She looks pissed and dejected and tired.

"I'm sorry," Tate says as she walks to the door.

Sadie doesn't turn to look at him or say good-bye. She quietly makes her parting remarks as she slips out the door. "Obviously, you're not sorry enough."

Poor Sadie. She feels completely defeated. I didn't mean to saddle her with this obligation. I wish I could help her. I wish there were something I could do.

seventeen

Sadie is going to have to live with the knowledge that I was a thief. My parents will find out and be devastated. I wonder what my grandmother will think of the fact that I was a kleptomaniac. I only stole from her one time. I took a bracelet from her jewelry box when I was visiting her four years ago. She asked me about it on my next visit. But I just acted like I didn't know anything. I guess I look like an honest person because she believed me. Only Sadie saw through me. Maybe because we spent so much time together. Or maybe we had a real and true connection.

I'm standing in Tate's front yard beside a rhododendron. My grandmother accidentally killed a rhododendron when I was a kid. She didn't catch its root rot in time. The whole thing died. When she realized she couldn't save it, she swore at it.

"You dying shit!" she'd yelled.

I'd never heard her swear before. "Maybe it will grow back," I'd told her.

"That's not how gardening works. After you murder a bush, it's dead forever."

"Sorry," I'd said.

"I don't think it's really anybody's fault. Root rot happens."

I hadn't thought about that rhododendron until right now. I'm surprised I can remember our conversation. Ready or not, it happens. I can see my grandmother and myself. She's at the mortuary. And before I have time to rethink my decision, I step into the gray tunnel and fly to her. It's the shortest trip yet. One moment I'm in a grassy yard, the next I'm falling through a ceiling, landing on carpet. I am in the absolute last place I want to be. My grandma and Aunt Claire are standing over my body, talking.

There is an unmistakable pull for me to be as close to my body as possible. But I resist it. I don't want to stand next to my body. Please, let me avoid ending up like Louise. Overcome with sadness, trapped by a potent connection to my lifeless corpse.

"She looks like she's sleeping," my grandmother says, sniffling.

A white sheet is draped over me, covering me all the way to the neck. I refuse to focus on my face. This is too real. Too sad.

"Nobody confronts this easily," Louise says. I can feel her presence beside me. "But it's one of the last times you'll see yourself. So you might consider this a final opportunity."

"I can't see it that way," I say.

I glance around the funeral home and feel sickened by all the decorative details. There are flower arrangements placed on every flat surface, and I can't smell any of them. The light is thin and dying, as if they are trying to disguise what the dead truly look like. I hear the sound of water, look out the glass doors, and notice a young boy leaning over a drinking fountain. A stream flows easily into his pink mouth. I turn away from this. Every small thing I see now is making me desperately sad. Because I used to drink water. I used to have a pink mouth.

"Don't stay too long," Louise says. "You don't want to use up all your time here."

"Don't worry," I say.

"This kills me," my grandmother says. "It absolutely kills me."

I put my arms around her and hug her from behind. "I'm okay. I'm still here."

"She looks lovely," Aunt Claire says. "I didn't realize her hair had gotten so long."

I finally look at myself. Somebody has pulled my hair forward over my shoulders and smoothed it out. Normally, on a good day, my hair had a natural wave to it. But today it's basically straight. I'm not wearing any makeup. I look so dead. I thought I might look like I was sleeping, but my skin is a waxy color. And my hands rest stiffly at my side. I turn my back and move so I stand between my grandmother and my body.

"I'm okay," I repeat, even though it's a lie. "I love you."

"We should be the ones to dress her," my grandmother says. "A lot of my friends have died as of late, and morticians are lousy at makeup application. We should do it. We know what Molly looks like. We should be the ones to fix her up."

"I agree," Aunt Claire says. "We can pick up her own makeup from the house."

"We can use this picture as a guide," my grandmother says, opening up her wallet. I look at the photo. It's two years old. I totally look like a child. Why doesn't my grandmother have a more current photo?

"We should go check on them," Aunt Claire says.

I know she means my parents. And I think that I should go too.

"I need to visit the restroom first," my grandma says.

I probably shouldn't follow her there. I wait outside. On the opposite side of the foyer, behind a set of French doors, a funeral is taking place. I look inside. The man who died is old. His family fills the chairs. A woman wearing a long black dress plays a sad song on the organ. I mean, it sounds like actual weeping, and not just a person, but maybe an elephant. Standing beside the casket is the man's twin. He seems happy. He waves energetically to all the grieving people. Weird. I'm glad I don't have a socially inappropriate twin.

My grandmother is still in the bathroom. Should I check on her? No. That's stupid. I keep watching the funeral. In two days I'm going to have a funeral. Everybody I love will be sitting in a room just like this one, singing, talking about me. And then I'll move to the next phase. What does that even mean? Halfway through the song, I watch the man's twin as he actually sits down on the closed bottom half of the casket. He must be mentally unstable. Nobody even reprimands him. The twin looks at me and smiles. Then he waves. Wait. He can see me? Okay, I'm an idiot. I realize I'm watching the dead man's soul.

After a few moments, his wife comes and signals with her arm for him to climb off the casket. He jumps down. The two of them link arms and stand next to the organist. There's only one casket, so this funeral isn't for both of them. She must have passed first. They must've just been reunited.

This isn't what my funeral is going to look like. I won't be happy. And Louise hasn't mentioned that anyone will be greeting me. Just like everybody else, I'm going to be sitting there totally depressed, bracing myself for the next phase.

Thunderous music drifts out of the organ. What a terrible choice of musical instrument. A saxophone would be better.

"You haven't been told everything," a voice says.

The voice doesn't sound like Louise's. I turn to look behind me. Nobody is there.

"I'm not Louise."

There's nobody with me in the hallway. I mean, I can't see anybody, but it does feel as if somebody else is here. Maybe it's some other soul at the mortuary. Maybe it's a helpful soul. Because the voice is right. I should know more things.

"Tell me what I haven't been told," I say.

There is a lot of silence. Then I hear a toilet flush.

"I can't help you unless you invite me to appear."

This could be a trick. But why would somebody try to trick me? It isn't like vampires plague the postlife. That's not what's going on.

"I only ask once to be invited."

I don't say anything. I'm not sure if I should invite this person. It feels like it's a woman. My mind goes to a piece of advice that my mother once gave me. She said if I ever became lost that I should look for a woman to help me. She said I shouldn't ask a man. So if a woman is trying to help me now, I should extend an invitation. Right?

"I promise I won't hurt you. I can help you," the voice says. "I'm harmless."

Wouldn't Louise have mentioned if there were souls to avoid? Whatever or whomever the voice belongs to is moving away from me. I can feel that. The growing distance panics me. I want to know more. And I definitely feel like I need help. I haven't been told enough. And I'm not happy with where things are headed.

"I invite you," I say.

Then I feel my soul being violently pulled out the door, down the green-carpeted steps, and into the parking lot.

Things feel wrong. I've made a mistake. "I take it back," I yell. "I uninvite you."

"No take-backs."

My soul doesn't stop at the parking lot. It's yanked down the street to a bridge. People are walking down the sidewalk enjoying the sunny day. Nobody can tell I'm being soul-jacked. A pigeon pecks at bread crumbs like it's a totally normal afternoon.

"Slow down!" I scream.

I wish I could see who I'm dealing with. Everything is happening so fast.

Suddenly, I'm sucked under the bridge, and I'm overwhelmed with a feeling of dread. Water flows past me. Can souls drown? Wait, I'm on top of the water. It's taking me somewhere. I try to calm down. We're approaching a park. Then I'm yanked into the grass. And dragged over a hill. I know where I am. I'm at the zoo. My soul doesn't stop. I zoom past the pens of goats and rabbits.

"I want to stop! Let go of me right now!" I say.

"No. I'm taking you to the snow cone stand," the voice says.

"That's a dumb place to take me. I can't eat a snow cone," I say. "And I really don't have time to hang out. My funeral is almost here."

"I know. That's why I found you. We're nearly out of time."

eighteen

I am in front of the snow cone stand. But since it's October, the small wooden shack is shuttered for the season.

"This is one of my favorite places," the voice says. "I came here as a child. A teenager. And once I was grown."

I remember this place. It's where the carnival sets up every year. The place where I won my stuffed peacock with Sadie and my family. It feels like I was just here.

"You like it here too," the voice tells me. "I can tell."

And then the voice isn't a voice anymore. It's a soul. A woman in her forties walks toward me. She's wearing clothes like I've seen my grandmother wear in photographs from her college days. Her pants flare at the bottoms, and her loose gypsy top drapes her thin frame in oversized ruffles. She has gray hair and sort of an angular and mischievous face. If I saw her at the carnival I'd think she was a fortune-teller.

This is the first soul besides Louise's that I've spoken with since I've been dead, and it's a little exciting. I wave at her, and when she waves back I notice that one of her long sleeves flaps in the wind. That's odd because a breeze doesn't make my clothes move. And unlike other souls, for example, her soul's skin has more color. Her peachy complexion actually looks healthy, practically alive. I'm a little confused, because maybe she isn't a soul. Maybe she's a clairvoyant person or a ghost chaser or something like that. But Louise said that none of those things were real.

"I thought you were a soul," I say. "But you look like you have a body."

She smiles at me. "It's part of what I know."

I'm curious to hear more, to find out what another soul has learned about being a soul.

"I'm eighty-five percent soul and fifteen percent body."

I've never thought of the connection between body and soul in terms of a percentage before.

"When you're alive, you're fifty percent soul and fifty percent body—for the most part. When you die, you become one hundred percent soul," she explains.

"I'm dead. So I'm one hundred percent soul."

"Well, I'm dead too. But I refuse to be just a soul."

I'd never even considered that an option. "How is that possible?" I ask.

She puts her finger to her mouth. "Don't ask me any questions," she warns. "You'll draw the attention of your soul's intake counselor. And then I won't be able to help you."

"My counselor won't let you help me," I say, trying to phrase my question as a statement.

"Counselors have an agenda. They tell you the minimum

amount of information, to limit your options so you'll do exactly what they want. It's all mind tricks and control games."

This makes sense. After showing me that chicken hatch, Louise has left me on my own to answer all my questions by myself. I don't have options.

"Tell me what you know," I say.

"Where do you want to start?"

"Being fifteen percent body means you can feel things," I say.

She nods. "I have a diminished sense of taste, touch, and smell. But, like you, like all souls before they cross, I have perfect hearing and sight."

I'm jealous. I can't taste, touch, or smell anything. And without this sort of intervention, I may never taste, touch, or smell anything ever again. My sensory future is beyond bleak.

"All souls have the potential to regain their other senses."

"My intake counselor should have told me this." My mind turns to Louise and her messy desk and reticent attitude. I'd assumed she was a little inept. But that's not it. Maybe that was an act. Maybe she doesn't want to answer any questions. I'll bet her job of guiding me to the next phase is much easier if I'm kept mostly in the dark. Like a total sheep, I have to follow everything she says.

"Like I said, sometimes counselors edit out a few details."

"This one seems rather big!"

"Well, it takes hard work to regain your senses. I've been working at it since my death almost forty years ago."

Just as with Louise, I'm reminded that I'm not just talking to a soul, but to a former human being. And upon realizing this, I become ravenously curious, wanting to know about her life and death and how she ended up uncrossed. But unless I want to alert Louise to the fact that I'm having this conversation, I can't ask any questions. I'm going to have to be a little patient and hope that she just tells me things.

"You probably have a name," I say. It takes effort to constantly be thinking in the form of statements.

"I'm Hilda."

She doesn't tell me her last name and I don't press. I want to know how she died, but I'm not sure if it's appropriate for a soul to fish for this information.

"You're probably wondering how I died. It's very natural for souls, especially newer souls, to be curious about this."

I nod.

"I died right over there," Hilda says. She points to the river.

"Under the bridge," I say. I remember the dark sensation I felt when I passed beneath it. That's what it was. I sensed Hilda's place of death.

"Yes, my body was swept under the bridge by the current. But I went into the river upstream. It was a car accident."

"Your car went into the river," I say.

"Yes, I was with my dog, Jackson. And I lost control."

I've lived here my whole life and never heard of that happening. Hilda must have been driving incredibly fast. I glance around for a dog or for any sign of a dog's soul. I'm still not sure how that works. It would be great if I could meet up with Hopkins again. Maybe his name is written on one of my clocks. I should check for that.

"Jackson survived. He was an excellent swimmer."

Hilda doesn't seem on the verge of tears about her death. If I were standing next to where Peppa had thrown me and the snake bit me, I would be a wreck. Maybe after forty years the pain dries up.

"All of our days are numbered. Nobody escapes death," Hilda says.

"Well, at least your dog survived," I say, smiling.

Hilda doesn't smile back. Maybe she wanted her dog to die.

I don't have time to get hung up on this. We need to keep things upbeat and move this conversation along. As we stand and talk, I feel this urgency. I need to learn things as quickly as I can. My funeral is around the corner.

"I want to know everything you know," I say. "In the postlife, information is delivered so slowly. I'm a smart person. A quick learner. Toss things at me as fast as you want."

Hilda raises her eyebrows. She seems slightly annoyed at my eagerness to quicken the pace.

"Why don't you tell me how you died?" Hilda asks. "You're so young."

I guess since she has shared, it's only polite for me to share too. "It's a sad story," I say. "I was on a date and fell off my horse and hit my head on a rock and got bitten by a snake." I don't mention that it was the bite to my butt that proved fatal. It makes my death seem a little comedic.

"That's awful," Hilda says. "How old are you, seventeen?"

"Sixteen," I say. Which will forever be my answer to that question.

"Sixteen. Unbelievable. Life is so unfair."

She stares down at me, pitying me for my young death.

"It is unfair," I say. But deep down I keep hold of this irrational hope that some time in the near future things are going to turn fair for me again.

"Follow me," Hilda says. "Let me show you something."

I follow her into the closed snow cone stand. The delivery window is boarded shut, and the side door is locked with two shiny metal padlocks. Hilda enters it like she owns the place. Inside, we find that everything is stored away for next season.

"You probably miss being able to touch and hold things," she says.

I nod. "Yes."

"Well, watch this."

Hilda mesmerizes me as she reaches up, grabs a cabinet knob, and pulls opens the wooden door. She knocks stacks of paper cones from the lower shelf and they tumble to the floor. Then she opens a second cupboard containing a row of snow cone syrups.

"I love making the bottles drip," Hilda says.

With the palm of her hand she presses the pump tops, making sweet liquid ooze down the sides of the bottles.

I want to ask her why she's trashing the snow cone stand. But I don't want my mind to transmit my question to Louise. I sort of understand why Hilda is doing this. It must feel amazing to make things move.

"You look like you're really enjoying yourself," I say. If I were fifteen percent body, I don't know that I'd waste my energy vandalizing a snack area. I think I'd go and touch things that mattered. Like the people I love.

"I can feel the cabinet's hardness and the syrups' stickiness," Louise says.

I want to ask her how, but I force myself to phrase this as a statement. "You must have had a good teacher to learn how to do this."

"I taught myself."

That's amazing. It never would occur to me to teach myself to feel things again. I'd just accepted that I'd lost that ability forever. But now I know better.

"I can teach you," Hilda says, "but it will take time."

I shake my head. "I don't have time. There are people I have to visit. I've got two life moments to relive. And I have to maintain an upbeat attitude the whole time or I'll bust more of my clocks."

Hilda seems entertained by my to-do list. "Molly, I see people make this mistake every day. They die. They're given a chore list. Then they race to finish it, and once they're done, they cross into a place where they never experience any real feeling again. Don't doom yourself to such a grim fate."

"Death just happens," I try to explain. "It's inevitable. We all meet this grim fate."

"Wrong!" Hilda says. She flings open another cupboard and sends a box of straws showering down on me. They pass through my soul and make pinging sounds as they land on the floor. "It's a lie that you have to cross and never feel again. I didn't cross, and look at where I ended up."

I'm not really itching to wind up in a seasonal snack hut. But I don't say this, because I'm also really intrigued. This means I could live in my house again. My bedroom. I could be around my parents. I could watch my brother and sister grow up.

"Molly, the first step in regaining your senses is that you must refuse to cross."

"I can't do that. My funeral is in two days. I think I have to cross."

"No, you don't. At your funeral, as your body is being interred, a door will open. You'll want to walk through it. It will feel like the right thing to do. But if you want to regain what you've lost, you must refuse it."

I keep thinking about my parents. The twins. My friends. Henry. Even Tate. I could remain a part of their lives. I like what Hilda is telling me. I think I want this.

"What's your destiny, Molly?"

"I'm not sure. Louise hasn't told me. I guess my job is to advance." But I really have no idea what the next phase holds for me. I look down at the snow cone cups littering the floor. I feel ashamed that I wasn't more successful in life. And that I died so ridiculously. "Maybe I'm getting what I deserve," I say, trying to explain.

"You're being way too hard on yourself. Nobody gets it right. You just do the best you can. Don't beat yourself up over a few poor choices."

I nod. It feels good to have her support.

"Let's skip to what matters now. How many clocks do you have left?" Hilda asks.

Wow. Hilda knows about the clocks. She has the postlife and its rules down. "Maybe sixty. But I might have lost a few more today," I say.

Hilda's eyes grow wide with surprise, and she opens a third cabinet, containing napkins. She takes a stack in her hands and tosses them up in the air. "That's not enough connections for a meaningful afterlife. You'll be very lonely if you cross."

She says this with such certainly that I have no doubt it's true. After she's finished tossing the napkins around, she walks up to me and puts her arm around my shoulder. I can't feel it, but I like the gesture. Louise doesn't even try to pretend that she cares about me in this way. But Hilda seems honestly invested in my eternal happiness. Hilda, unlike Louise, doesn't just see me as part of her job. I feel lucky to have met her.

"Wouldn't you rather stay and watch your family? All the exciting things that happen—you could be right in the same room with them."

I think about this option. Of course I want that.

"Come outside," Hilda says.

We exit the little shed and we're out in the bright afternoon. A blue jay lands on a fence nearby. I'm struck by a strange feeling. I'm lucky that I can still see the color blue. I should soak it up. Then I realize something. I don't know how I know this, but I do: once I cross, I'm not going to be able to see colors. I'm going to lose my last two senses.

I want to ask Hilda whether or not this is true. No. I can't ask any questions. I'll save this for Louise.

"Peeps!" Hilda cries. "Peeps!"

The bushes near the fence line rustle. A huge gray tomcat emerges and struts toward us.

"You just called that cat," I say. This means Hilda has a voice.

"I can teach you to have a voice again. You can't have conversations, but you can make sounds. You can make your presence known." She places both hands on my shoulders and looks me in the eye, but I can't feel her. "Molly, if you want to cross over and have a job and be separated from all the people who love you and wait for them to die and hope you somehow are still able to stay connected, go ahead and take that chance. But I know the risks involved, especially for a soul with so few connections left. When I come across souls poised to cross, but who know nothing of the risks, I arrive to show them other ways to exist."

The tomcat, Peeps, rubs his body against Hilda's legs. She bends over and scratches his belly. Static electricity ripples across his fur.

"I'm not sure," I say. "I feel like I should at least mention this to my intake counselor."

Hilda throws her arms over her head.

"That's a horrid idea. Your counselor is biased. It's her job to help you cross. Without a doubt, she'll discourage you from becoming an uncrossed soul."

Hilda drops to her knees and pets the cat with both hands. Watching this, I can't help thinking of my own cat,

Hopkins. I miss being able to touch things. I want to feel again.

"If you come tomorrow, I can teach you how to touch something small," Hilda said.

"Like a cat?"

"Sure, I can teach you how to touch a cat. Or a person."

My mind leaps to Henry, which surprises me a little. "That means a person could feel me, and I could feel them," I say.

"Yes, but you'll barely be able to feel the person, and same for them. You'd just be starting."

"Tomorrow it will be hard for me to make it here. I have to relive my last two life moments," I explain.

Hilda sighs. "That's too bad. Fresh souls learn the fastest."

"One day of freshness can't make that much difference."

"Oh, but it does. Think of how quickly bread grows stale."

Well, I can't *not* relive my moments. And I need to visit Tate. And my parents again. Maybe I can come by afterward. "I have things to do, and I can't abandon my family and friends during their grief," I insist.

"Molly, if you don't cross, you'll be able to be around your family and friends for the rest of their lives."

"I hadn't thought of it that way." But at the same time, I really want to relive those moments. To feel alive again is so thrilling. So worth it. I feel a tug. I can tell it's my parents. And I want to see them again. I miss them.

"I have two life moments left," I tell her.

Hilda looks excited. "Have you learned the trick of extending your moment?"

"Pick a really long one?" I ask. "Like where I'm standing in line or something?"

"No. It's actually simple. All you do is anchor your vision."

"I don't know how to do that."

"You look at something in the room where you want to stay and you don't look away. Focus on the object and you don't have to leave."

"I have to go," I say. "I'll think about everything you've told me. Thank you." I see the tunnel forming next to me. I need to step into it.

"Molly, remember, you must decide before your funeral if you don't want to cross. You can't stay for the lowering of the casket into the ground. You must leave before then."

"I'll think about it," I repeat.

"If you don't cross, then I can help you. I promise."

And hearing those last words, I am flung into the tunnel. Gray all around me. Zooming to what I think is my house. When I break into the sky I realize that death has exhausted me. I didn't know a soul could get this tired. I go to my bedroom, find my bed, and curl up on it. It's dark outside. It felt like I was only with Hilda for a few minutes. But hours and hours have gone by. I don't know how that happened. But I guess it doesn't matter. I focus on where I am now. I can still hear all the familiar sounds in the house. The dishwasher running. Our old refrigerator humming with effort. Hopkins purring.

"I miss you, Hopkins," I say.

I don't have any idea if I'll see him again after my funeral. Nobody has explained how animal souls work. Hilda's dog isn't around in soul form. It doesn't seem right that I'm expected just to leave everybody behind. Hopkins leaps up on the bed expectantly. I want to believe he can sense that I'm here. He walks toward me and flops down, exposing his belly as if he wants me to pet it. But I can't do that. I don't know how.

After I leave everyone, I wonder if I'll be able to stay in touch with how they're doing. I know I won't be *with them*. But maybe my mind will be so powerful and my soul so curious that frequent updates about their well-being will just arrive. If I can't, if crossing over means that I leave everybody I love, then is it even worth it? What's the point of existing if you are denied access to every single person you care about? And it's here, teetering on the verge of leaving everybody I love, that I realize I can't do it. No. No. No.

The people I love are here. I am here. What's the point of leaving them? Without love, what do I have? I'm exhausted. I need something to lift me. A life moment. And I don't want anything hard or challenging. Give me something happy. Let's stick with this theme. Deliver me to a moment of love.

nineteen

I'm not sure how I ended up in Henry's room, but I'm here, sitting on his shag rug, stirring my hands through it. It doesn't feel like I'm dead. My senses have returned, and I can feel everything perfectly. Backlit, Henry holds his saxophone with both hands and leans his head forward a little, cheeks inflated. How come I've never noticed the sexual nature of the saxophone before? Wait. I wanted a life moment that dealt with love. And I'm in Henry's bedroom? Wasn't that lust?

Henry pulls the horn from his mouth and sets the instrument in a stand beside his bed. Love. Lust. I think I feel both. I think *he* feels both.

"It's soulful," I say, staring up at him with that new and exciting and painful realization that this is more than just a high school make-out session. It is the beginning of something important.

"Thanks," Henry says.

He looks sad as he sits down next to me on the carpet. I think he already loves me. Is that why he broke up with

192

Melka? Because he knew I was coming over to his house that night and he wanted to make out with me? I grab my wrist with my hand. I can feel my pulse. I can feel the rhythm of blood pumping through me. Life. It's coursing through me and it's wonderful. But I can't just sit and feel my own pulse all night. I look up at Henry.

"You're so quiet," I say. I wish he would tell me what he's thinking.

"I'm thinking about Melka," he says.

"Oh, God." This is our last time together. I don't want to hear about Melka. I wish I had been bolder. I wish I had told him how I was feeling.

"So you've heard," he says.

I drop my wrist and shake my head. I stare into his face, into his eyes. They are so sad. He takes his glasses off so I can look directly into his eyes. No glass barrier. I had all these empty seconds where we were just looking at each other, totally connected. I could have asked him anything. I could have told him anything. Instead, I just sat there, losing myself somewhere between Henry's black pupils and hazel irises. It's amazing that you can know someone for years and years and suddenly they can look so different, so *sexy*. I can't believe that I didn't know this was the real thing.

He finally speaks. "I broke up with Melka."

I swallow. And continue to stare.

"Oh," I say. Sounding so sorry, even though I'm not.

"It wasn't going anywhere," he says.

I will be dead in a matter of days. Why would I start to

fall in love with somebody days before I die? This won't be going anywhere either. "It has to be going somewhere," I say.

His face moves closer to my face, and when I sense his breath approaching my mouth, I close my eyes. At the beginning of summer I made a promise that I would not waste my junior year. Everything I did had to matter. Because high school is important. This was supposed to be the year I made my mark.

Henry laughs. I open my eyes.

"You're laughing at me?" I ask. Why can't we just kiss? Why do I have to relive the awkward parts?

"It's your face," he says.

I still can't believe that he laughed at my face.

"You look cute when you close your eyes," he says.

I swat his leg pretty hard. This is so uncomfortable to relive; I am a terrible flirt.

"Do you want to stop?" he asks.

No, I think. My whole life will be stopping in four days. Let's go. Let's go.

"Do *you* want to stop?" I ask.

He stands up, and my whole body is flooded with disappointment.

"What kind of music do you like?" He walks to his desk, opens his laptop, and clicks through files.

"I'm new to jazz," I say.

He turns around and wags his finger at me like he's disappointed. "You're missing out. You want to hear Lee Konitz?"

I nod. Henry's right. I'll be missing out on everything.

"Maybe you want to hear Jackie McLean?"

I nod again. "Both of them," I say. This will be the last time that my body and soul will ever hear jazz music.

While his back is to me, I lift a low-hanging sheet so I can peek under his bed. I see a flash drive. A sock. Then I see Melka's keys. Why am I doing this? I reach under the bed and snag them. I settle the sheet back in place. As I slide the keys into my front pocket I'm surprised by how excited I feel. I always knew I had a problem. I always knew I couldn't stop. But reliving it this way makes me feel like my problem was bigger than I realized.

"You like this?" he asks.

I nod again, and he sits down next to me. His thin body feels strong as he pulls me toward his lap. He runs his hands through my hair over and over again, and we just keep staring at each other. This is young love, I think. This is where it happened. This isn't just where Henry Shaw fell in love with me; this is where I fell in love with him too.

We lean toward each other until his lips touch my lips. After three gentle presses I feel his tongue. He pulls away from my mouth, and my eyes pop open. We're just looking at each other. Watching each other breathe. We start again. This time we aren't as gentle. We kiss desperately. Like it's a life-sustaining activity. I am going to miss him so much. Especially if I cross. His hands reach around my waist. *Fast. Fast. Fast.* They want to tug at my shirt. I can feel that they want to do that. But he doesn't let his hands go anywhere under my clothes. His fingers crawl along my back. We kiss. We kiss. His mouth is on my neck. We begin falling backward into a horizontal position. When I notice the base of a brass floor lamp next to my head, I realize that this moment is ending.

The sounds of songs I've only heard once, instruments I can't quite identify, float out of the speakers on Henry's shelf. Then I hear his front door slam shut. Melka. The wall holding his band plaques shakes, and we fly apart. I lift myself until I'm on my knees, swooning from the last make-out session of my life.

"I'm supposed to be in your kitchen!" I whisper, panicked and a little dazed.

"You look so guilty," Henry says. "It's okay."

"Kitchen!" I whisper again, standing up, urgently making my way through the hall, down the stairs. No. No. No. I want things to end now. But they don't. They play out the way they are supposed to play out.

"Melka!" I say. Her blond hair is swept into a messy ponytail. She is the last person I want to see right now. The last.

"Molly Weller?" Melka says. The way she utters my name makes it sound like a criminal act.

I don't say anything else. How could things end so badly? How can I fall in love on a Wednesday night and die on a Saturday afternoon?

"Dis? Dis? Is how you treat me?" Melka asks. She squints, and tears gather in the corners of her eyes. "You git wit Molly Weller?"

When Melka speaks my name the second time, she sounds disgusted.

"We were studying," I lie. "I've got to go."

"Melka, why are you here?" Henry asks. He looks beyond uncomfortable. "We broke up."

Why couldn't I have stayed and asked what was going on? I could have spent the last three days of my life being in love with Henry, instead of trying to get over him.

"Yesterday," Melka says. Her tears have intensified and turned into sobbing.

I know I said I was leaving, but I continue to stand there. Once I leave Henry, it's over. This is the second-to-last time we'll talk. I want to stay as long as possible.

"I left keys to my bike lock," Melka says. "Maybe in your room."

Henry nods. "Okay. You can go look. I haven't seen any keys. I'll go with you."

"Bye!" I say, racing to leave. You can't undo anything. If I could have, I would have thrown my arms around him and told him how I really felt. I would have done something, said something, made something happen that was meaningful. I can feel the sensations that are pulsing through me begin to fade. My pulse. My breath. My taste. My heat.

The moment is ending for me. No. I don't want to leave. Wait. This doesn't have to end right now. I *can* stay longer.

I remember Hilda's advice. "Focus on an object, and you don't have to leave."

I need an object. Melka's ponytail. I lock my eyes on it, and as it travels back to Henry's room, so do I. Gone are all the physical sensations that accompanied my life moment. But that doesn't matter. I'm still in the scene, learning about what happened after I left.

"I don't know where your keys are," Henry says.

"I left them here!" Melka says, panicked and insistent.

"I'm sorry," he says. "Calm down."

"How can I calm down? You look at Molly Weller like you love her!" Melka says.

Henry doesn't correct her. He doesn't say anything. Oh my god. Henry Shaw loves me.

"You and I broke up," Henry says.

"But you said we're still friends," Melka says. "Good friends."

I stand in the corner and watch Melka's ponytail. I wish I could focus on Henry's face, but that would mean that I leave the moment.

"We are still good friends," Henry says.

"We were supposed to go to Salt Lake City. You were going to drive me to visit my cousin."

That's so weird. Henry should refuse. You're supposed to get distance after a breakup. I've never even had one and I know this basic rule. And how is it possible that Melka has a cousin in Salt Lake City?

"I'll drive you down to see her," Henry says. But he certainly looks like he doesn't want to drive her down.

"She's the only relative I have in the United States. I want to see her before I go," Melka says.

"I'll take you," Henry says.

Then Melka crumples to the floor.

"Please, don't," Henry says.

"I hate it here," Melka says. "I don't have any friends. I only had you. And now I don't have dat. Who will I eat lunch with? I miss my family. My friends. Dis experience is terrible! I am all alone."

Henry sits down beside her. "I'll eat lunch with you. You're not all alone."

And then he hugs her, and for a fraction of a second I look at him, breaking my focus on her ponytail, and then I'm falling out of the picture. They stay in the bedroom and I go somewhere else. This is all so confusing. Henry should have just told me that Melka was an emotional wreck. He should have explained things to me over the garbage can in the cafeteria. Or called me.

And then I remember that he *did* try to explain things to me over the garbage can in the cafeteria. And he *did* call me. The day I died. And I didn't take his call. I should have. But I didn't know what was at stake. I thought I'd have more time. Love, in my head, was supposed to happen differently. Never for a moment did I think I would die.

twenty

My moment is over. I'm back in my bedroom. Henry is gone. Maybe forever. So many times I woke up and looked at my ceiling and wanted to go back to sleep. Or I woke up and wished I didn't have to go to school or help do yard work or some other undesirable chore. A lot of my life slipped away while I wasn't doing anything.

When I hear my mother's voice, I'm pulled into a heightened state of awareness. "Of course you can see her room."

This is great news! Sadie is here. She's really going to help me. She's come to my room to get all the things I stole so my family won't find out that I'm a thief. It only takes a second for me to realize what this means. Henry is here, too. Because Sadie told Tate that Henry had agreed to help. Henry Shaw may be standing outside my window right now! I hurry to see if he really is there.

He is! This is the happiest I've felt in a long time. Look at him! Uh-oh. Henry may be an outstanding saxophone player, but he's terrible at crouching. I watch as he tumbles into the small boxwood hedge beneath my window. I wish

I could tell him how I feel. I wish I could say something. Do something. He reaches up and pulls off the screen covering my window. Is he going to try to climb inside my room? He can't do that. It's impossible. Because I bent something structurally important last spring and now my window only opens halfway. Oh my god. If Henry misjudges something and gets stuck in my window, my parents are going to think he's a stalker. What if they're so disoriented by their grief that they call the police on him? Could that damage my future connection with him? Is it normal to have these issues after you die?

I lean out the window. "My window is broken!" I yell. "Stay in the bushes!"

If I'd studied with Hilda I'd know how to fix this. I try to keep my commands simple. Why did she bother showing me that it's possible to make syrup bottles drip? I need to be able to communicate with the living. That's the first thing they should teach dead people.

"Bushes are safe!" I try hard to use my energy to rustle the boxwood or make a wood chip fly at him to frighten him off, but nothing works. "Window equals police." I don't know if that's true, but sometimes people respond to dramatic statements.

"This is one of the stupidest things I've ever done in my life," Henry says.

"True!" I say. "Leave! My room is no place for you!"

I look around to ascertain the state of my belongings. Whoa. People have just entered my room. Grandma and Aunt Claire. And they're taking my things. That seems premature. I know I don't need them anymore, but it feels inappropriate to swoop in and snatch them right before my funeral. I watch as they set out all of my makeup on my dresser and sort through it. Oh. I remember. They're gathering my makeup so they can prepare my body. I look at the unmade bed and the discarded clothes on the floor. It's embarrassing to count five pairs of dirty underwear draped around my laundry basket. Alive, I didn't feel like I was a slob, but looking at things now, I realize I should have treated my room like a sanctuary instead of a locker room equipped with a television.

My grandmother picks up some hideous purple nail polish that I bought as a joke to decorate my toenails in eighth grade.

"Should we paint her fingernails?" Aunt Claire asks.

"Don't bury me with purple fingernails!" I plead.

This is so stressful. If I could just tell them—if I could just let them know what I want—death would be so much easier. I should have kept an in-case-I-die journal. And in it I should have left detailed instructions. And I should have kept a current photo of myself with it. And a list of all the makeup I use, which isn't much. This entire postdeath catastrophe could have been avoided.

"I think she only painted her nails for Halloween," Grandma says.

That's not entirely true, but close enough. "Nice call, Grandma."

"What about perfume?" Aunt Claire asks.

I can't look at this anymore. Where Aunt Claire found

the bottle she's holding, I'm not quite sure. I never wore perfume. And even if I did, you don't put that stuff on dead teenagers. What's wrong with her? Sadie needs to hurry up. I can hear her voice. She's talking to my mother in the living room. Just get in here. She doesn't need to talk to my mother. They're not *that* close. And why is Henry still in my boxwood? He's smart; he should be able to sense danger. Now I hear something else. The doorbell. I leave my room to see who it is. It's Tate. He agreed to help after all.

My mother lets him inside, and I watch them hug. He looks sad. She looks miserable. And Sadie is anxious beyond belief. She has a backpack slung over her shoulder.

"So you don't mind if I visit her room?" she asks.

That my room has become the most popular destination on the block creeps me out.

My mother tilts her head back, and I watch tears form at the corners of her eyes and slip down her face. "Spend as much time as you need."

They hug, and I feel a strong twinge of jealousy. I wish I could be the one hugging my mother. Sadie turns toward my bedroom, and my mother stops her. "Wait. Doesn't she have some of your things?"

Sadie flips back around. She looks startled. "I, uh, don't know what she has in her room." She stumbles when she talks. She's afraid that my mother already knows.

"She's got your shoes. Remember?" my mother says. "You should probably take those now."

Sadie nods, and I watch her face relax in relief. "Right," she says.

"I haven't gone through her things yet," my mother says. "I'll need to do that. Soon."

Sadie returns to my mother's side and hugs her again. "I think that can wait. You should take as long as you want. And if you want me to help, I will."

My mother sniffles. "I should just put a day on the calendar and commit to it. Otherwise, I'm going to let it turn into a shrine. I'll never touch it. It will stay the way Molly left it. Forever."

That actually sounds good, I think. Because If I don't cross, I'll be able to surround myself with my stuff. It will be a lot like being alive. Except different. I feel a slight urge to return to my bedroom. Panic shoots through me. What if Grandma has spotted Henry in the bushes?

When I get there I see that nobody has discovered Henry. They're finalizing my makeup. "This is her blush," my grandma says. "Remember the photo I showed you?"

But I don't wear blush. That was just a free sample that I got at the mall. "Mom!" I call. "Can we get Grandma a more recent photo? She's going to make me look like a middle-school student, or possibly a child prostitute." It's the last time anybody is going to see me. I want to look natural, like myself.

My mother doesn't appear. It seems insane that a couple of days ago I could call for her anywhere in the house and she'd come to me. She was my mother. Now I don't know if I'm ever going to see her again. I cannot imagine a future without my mother; I cannot lose her clock. Shouldn't Louise be keeping track of this for me? Isn't that her job?

"You still have your mother. Your father. Your grandma. Sadie. Henry. And the people who matter most," Louise says.

If I were somebody's counselor, I wouldn't appear and disappear without any warning. I'd try my hardest to be a nurturing presence and say things like "I'm back" or "I'm leaving, and you can expect me back in an hour."

"After this, I want to go check on them myself," I say. I trust her, but I still want to verify what she's saying. After talking to Hilda, I'm not really sure that Louise is as invested in my outcome as I originally thought. I'm just one of many souls. It doesn't really matter to her where I end up.

"You're always free to return to the transition room," Louise says.

"That place with the clocks and your desk has a name?" I ask. "You never told me that."

"There's a sign on the door," Louise says.

She still should have told me that.

"Thanks," I say. But I'm not really thankful at all. I'm annoyed. Louise has been constantly withholding information. Watching that dumb chicken hatch was a total waste of my time. Louise isn't trying to strengthen me. Hilda was right. Louise wants to keep me in the dark so that I'll follow exactly what she says, because that's the easiest option for her.

"How many people do I have left?" I ask. "What's the exact number?"

"It hasn't been a good day for lasting eternal connections," Louise says.

Of course this would be her answer.

"In your list of people that I have left, you didn't mention Aunt Claire," I say. "Why not? Have I lost Aunt Claire?"

"Not yet," Louise says. "But you might soon. I'm sorry."

This startles *and* angers me. First, I don't think that Louise is sorry at all. Second, I like my aunt Claire. "We have a great connection!"

"Calm down," Louise says. "It's not always about what you did. Sometimes it's about what they did. Sometimes alignment becomes unaligned."

"But I haven't lost her yet?" I ask.

"Right," Louise says. "But there's a crack."

She never mentioned that the clocks cracked before they ruptured. "Are you sure you've given me all the information I need?"

I watch as Aunt Claire and my grandmother sort through my lip pencils. "I don't use those anymore," I explain. "I bought a bunch on sale but they're too dark."

"This looks like mauve," my grandma says. "I don't think I've ever seen Molly wear mauve."

"Let's just take the whole haul," Aunt Claire says. "We might need the options."

"This is so morbid," I tell Louise. "Can't you help me reach them and tell them what to do? There's got to be a way." My mind flashes to Hilda. She'd probably know.

"Have you thought about your last life moment?" Louise asks.

I cannot believe she is bringing that up right now. "I am comforting my family! And Henry Shaw, who happens to love me and is currently sitting in my boxwood hedge," I snap.

"It's great that you visited Henry," Louise says. She seems happy about it.

"Yeah, it is great. And you were right. He did break up with Melka. Turns out, we started to fall in love the night we kissed. Were you aware of that? And now none of that matters, because I'm dead. That's right. Everything sucks worse. Because in that life moment, I learned that I had screwed up the only important relationship I will ever have. I ruined it. Are you satisfied? Does it make you happy that I relived that life moment and got some clarity?" My anger at the situation is now redirected toward Louise.

"Your death doesn't make me happy, Molly. But we all die."

She's already said that once, and she doesn't need to say it again. Hearing it doesn't make me feel any better.

"In your moment with Henry you sought clarity. You gained something."

I don't feel like I *gained* anything. And the only reason I learned anything useful is that I followed Hilda's advice on how to stay in the moment. Without it, I wouldn't have known how to eavesdrop on Henry and Melka.

"For your last life moment, I really want to encourage you to confront a fear. Get as much clarity as you can while you still have the chance."

More clarity? This advice feels cryptic and oddly manipulative, and it totally ignores my stated preoccupations. "If you think you know which life moment I should relive, why don't you just tell me?"

"I can't instruct you that way," Louise says.

"Right," I say. "You can only give me enough information to make me feel doomed and flawed. Thanks."

"If being in your house with your family is too hard for you, you can always go somewhere else for a little while," Louise says.

Just as she finishes telling me this, my grandmother bursts into tears, and Sadie enters my bedroom.

"I can't just leave them grieving like this," I say. "They need me."

Louise shakes her head. "As shallow as this may sound, their wounds will heal."

I watch as Sadie hugs my grandmother. I wonder if the tables were turned I would have driven to Sadie's house and gone into her bedroom and hugged her grandmother. I'd like to think I would have done that.

"My parents will never get over me," I say. Hilda was right. Clearly, Louise has an agenda and wants me to cross. She sees how depressed and grief-stricken we all are, and she's not even suggesting I could stay.

"Your parents will keep on living," Louise says. "The twins won't replace you, but it will give your mom and dad new experiences. They will find new joys."

"Stop!" I tell Louise. I try to keep my focus on what's happening in my room.

"I told Sadie she could spend a few minutes alone in Molly's room," my mother says.

"We've got what we need," Aunt Claire says. "We're headed to the mortuary now." She's well stocked with random bits of makeup that I never intended to wear. But I am relieved she seems to have forgotten an entire bag. Maybe it will make her go light on my final makeover.

My grandma picks a garment bag up from my bed. These must be the clothes that I'm going to get buried in. What are they? My mother let my grandmother choose my burial clothes? My mother's grief must be debilitating. Because we both know that my grandma has no correct impulses when it comes to fashion.

"Thank you," my mother says. "I'm sure Molly would appreciate all your efforts to make her look her best."

"Yes," I say. "I do. But can we get her a more recent picture? And tell them about the lip pencils? And blush? And she forgot my blush brush. If you apply it with your fingers it can leave smudge marks."

"This is how you comfort your family?" Louise asks. "By obsessing about your burial appearance?"

I am done with Louise Davis. She's rotten. "I've got this covered. Really. I don't need to see you again until the funeral."

"You need to be careful," Louise says. "You don't want to say something wrong in anger."

"Wrong?" I am beyond pissed off at Louise. "I want you to leave. There's nothing *wrong* about that."

"Molly, if you phrase that statement like a commandment, you might unintentionally banish me."

That sounds like pure bliss.

"I have that kind of power?" I ask.

"You're a soul, Molly. You contain tremendous power."

"I'm sick of you, Louise. You're vague. You're unhelpful. You're depressing. You're bossy. Maybe we should take a break and meet up later. I'll come find you in the transition room."

"Don't do it," Louise says. "You'll regret it."

I will never regret this. As soon as I've made up my mind, I feel a powerful ripple of something trip through me. And I understand it. I, Molly Weller, have the power to make commandments. And I want to use it right now. "Louise Davis, I command you to leave. Don't find me. I'll find you."

She doesn't say anything to try to talk me out of it. She just goes. It's as if she's been vaporized. And as soon as she disappears, I feel liberated. I watch as everybody leaves my room except for Sadie. After she shuts the door, she races to the window and opens it. I notice that it stops midway. She tugs at it, trying to coax it open, but it won't budge. "It's broken," Sadie calls down to Henry. "You just stay there and I'll hand you everything."

She is an amazing friend. She flings open one of my dresser drawers and starts pawing through it. She has fantastic judgment, and selects stolen lipstick tubes, socks, key chains. She spots Melka's bicycle keys and grabs those too. Then she races to the window.

"Round one," she says, dumping all the contents out the window.

As Henry picks the bicycle keys up, I can tell he recognizes that they're Melka's. I feel so terrible. I don't want him to think poorly of me. Ruining his impression of me would damage our connection, I'm certain. I turn my attention back to Sadie. The pressure is getting to her, and she's racing through my room like a tornado, overlooking a ton of the stuff I stole. I've got a box in the back of my closet. And the pack of playing cards from my dad's convenience store. And her ring. I need to help her, but I don't know how to do that.

"Looks like you could use some instruction."

I turn to snap at Louise and remind her that I commanded her to leave, but then I realize I'm not looking at Louise. It's Hilda.

"Yes!" I say. I'm so relieved and excited that a helpful soul has arrived. "I need to tell Sadie what to do in simple commands. Or I need to write something on the mirror in lipstick. Or maybe spell something out with my socks."

Hilda laughs at me. Hard. But that makes sense. My suggestions are ridiculous. Why am I making everything so difficult? I should ask Hilda to communicate with Sadie for me. "Can you tell her things for me?"

"No," Hilda says. But then she smiles. "I'm going to give you a suggestion that's going to change everything for you."

Hilda needs to hurry. Sadie looks like she's winding up.

"Don't try to guide your friend. That's so inefficient," Hilda says. "Possess her."

"What?" I ask. This idea seems creepy and impolite.

"The best way to accomplish the things you need to do is to jump into Sadie's body and do them yourself. Possess her."

"I don't think I can do that," I say. I watch Sadie as she futilely rummages through my sock drawer.

"It doesn't harm anybody," Hilda says.

"It feels wrong," I say.

"Actually, it feels fantastic. All your senses will return. It's just like being alive."

"Hurry up!" Henry says. He's standing below my window, reaching his arms up, stretching his hands into my room.

"I could talk to Henry?" I ask.

"You could do anything you want. Should I tell you how it works?"

Do I want that? Yes, I want that. It is so weird to want that! "But what if I'm not any good at it?" I have enormous doubts and fears that it's not going to work.

"You have an aptitude for possession. I can tell. Everything I know about you has convinced me that you will do a marvelous job."

I know I shouldn't want to do this. But it feels like the only option I've got left.

twenty-one

Hilda tells me that possessing a body is like diving. She says I should imagine that Sadie is a pool of water and I need to enter her by making one powerful plunge.

I bring my arms out in front of me and press my hands together to form a point, like I'm literally going to dive. Sadie is on her hands and knees, clawing underneath my bed in a desperate attempt to find anything I've stolen. What started out as a calculated operation to scout for looted items has taken a turn toward chaos.

Standing over her, I aim my pressed hands at her back. And when I finally leap, I do so with every ounce of energy that I have. Much like the momentum I feel when the gray tunnels transport me, entering Sadie's body is accompanied by a rush of speed. My soul overtakes her, and suddenly I am Sadie Dobyns. Holy crap. I can feel the carpet underneath my bed. And I have a mouth again. I can speak! And Henry is outside my window. I jump up and race to him.

I can't stop myself from sticking my head out the window and sucking in huge breaths of air.

"The air smells so fresh and amazing!" I say.

"What are you doing?" Henry asks. "Are you done?"

I stare down at him. He's reaching up to take something, but I am not holding anything. I reach Sadie's hand—*my hand*—out the window and touch his fingers. It makes me feel electric and alive, and it's so thrilling that I never want to let go of him.

"I think the neighbor saw me," Henry says.

"Mr. Powell has terrible vision. My dad says he's legally blind. Don't worry. He probably thinks you're just a dog," I say with Sadie's voice.

Henry looks perplexed and finally pulls his hand away. "Is this everything?" he asks. "This might sound weird, but I think Molly took Melka's bike keys."

This panics me a little. Even a small shift in his opinion of me could strain our connection and damage his clock. I need to say something to clear my name.

"Let's not blame Molly for being a little flawed. We all take things," I say.

Henry looks even more confused than before and arranges the items in his courier bag and begins to zip it shut.

"I feel like I didn't even know Molly," Henry says.

My heart sinks. How can he say that? He should *not* be questioning our connection.

"She was great!" I say. "Some people are more complex than others."

"I think we should finish this up," Henry says. "And I wasn't trying to judge Molly. I really cared about her. She was . . ." He takes a short, meditative pause. ". . . great."

It's amazing to me that after the moment of my death I can still continue to experience so many terrible things. Henry and I should have had a chance. We should have had the opportunity to fall totally and completely in love. Who decided that one of us had to die?

"She's probably still great," I say. "She probably isn't that far away."

"Yeah," Henry says. "Sometimes it feels like she's still around."

"Are things okay in there?" my mother calls.

My mother. My mother is on the other side of the door. I speed toward it. After I throw it open, I wrap my arms around her. I smell her. Lilacs. Baby powder. Cinnamon. Dryer sheets. My mother.

"I know it's hard," my mother says, "It seems impossible that she's gone."

I can't let go of her. I won't. I am sobbing. We're both sobbing. "It's not fair," I say. "People should have a chance to say good-bye."

My mother holds me tightly. "We still have the funeral."

My funeral. As soon as my mother says these words, I become aware that I've made my decision. I can't cross. I can't leave her. Leave my family. Leave Sadie. Leave Henry. Leave my life. Never. I won't do it.

"Okay," my mother says, lightly pulling away from me. "How much longer do you need? Tate just showed up, and

215

I think it would be nice if we gave him Molly's invitation to the Sweetheart Ball. She would have wanted that."

What? I don't want that. I've changed my mind. Henry should be my date. Now that I have clarity and understand how Henry and I feel about each other, the idea of asking Tate seems completely wrong. Because I don't love Tate. And I need to keep my connection to Henry as strong as possible. This Sweetheart Ball invitation must be corrected.

"I think Molly wanted to ask Henry," I say.

Using her thumbs, my mother wipes away her tears. "No, she wanted to ask Tate. She wasn't sure where things were going with Henry. We'd been their neighbors when they were kids and they hadn't always gotten along."

Where did that idea come from? We got along fantastically. Until his friend said I had cooties and he stopped playing with me. And then he moved. I shake my head, because I totally disagree. I know better now. "No. I think she saw more of a future with Henry."

My mother laughs. "You remind me so much of Molly right now. It's uncanny."

If only I could tell her that I am Molly. I wish that I could. But it would be unfair to mess with her mind. She's fragile. Plus, she'd never believe it and end up thinking Sadie was crazy. Nobody would believe this. Even I barely believe it, and I'm the one currently possessing my former best friend's body.

"I'll give you a few more minutes," my mother says. "You shouldn't stay in here by yourself for too long. People should grieve together."

"Wait. Where's Dad?" I ask.

"What?" my mother asks.

It feels too strange to call my father by his first name. I try again. "Where's Molly's dad?"

My mother swallows hard. "At the store. Sometimes work helps people mend."

I am instantly pissed to hear that my father has abandoned my mother. This won't do. This won't do at all. My mother walks down the hallway toward the kitchen, and I reenter my room. This first thing I do is hurry to the window so I can look at Henry again. But he's already gone back to the car. I can hear Tate's voice in the other room. This operation is supposed to be ending. But I'm not ready. I race to find Sadie's ring. And the playing cards. And a few other random things I stole. I stuff them into Sadie's backpack. Except for the ring. I slide that onto her finger. No. That's stupid. What if my mother notices it? Then Sadie will have to explain that it's hers. And how will she explain why it's in my room? I slide it off and put it into her backpack, along with everything else. Then I get out my stationery. It's not too late to write a few good-bye letters.

"Sadie?" my mother calls. "Tate is here."

I do not have time to talk with Tate. I need to write my final thoughts down for everybody I love, so I scribble furiously. I write a note to my father. My mother. Aunt Claire. My grandma. Tate. Henry. Ruthann. Joy and Sadie. I want to offer them each a final message. One last thing from me they can keep. I struggle to use my best handwriting. I shove them all into the backpack. Then I write in big

217

letters, *Your ring is in the backpack. And I wanted to ask Henry to the Sweetheart Ball.*

"Done," I say.

I can hear my mother walking down the hall.

"Sadie?" she says.

I want to go back into the hallway and hug her again. To touch her and smell her and talk to her. I miss her so much. But I don't have time.

Wait. I have a problem. I don't know how to unpossess Sadie.

Hilda should be here still, right? "Hilda," I say. "I'm finished." She doesn't answer. Of course she doesn't. Because she's a soul and I'm a person now. Which means I can't see her. I focus really hard to see if she's sending me a sign. But my room looks like my room, and I don't notice anything. I really should have thought of this complication *before* I possessed Sadie. I glance around and mentally say good-bye to everything, hoping that will do that trick. But it doesn't. Hilda should have foreseen this issue. Why do souls intending to help me give me such minimal information? I don't know how to jump out of Sadie. I attempt to undive out of her. Nothing happens. Maybe I need to command my spirit and Sadie's body to separate using my voice.

"I am finished possessing you," I say.

Nothing happens.

My mother knocks on my door.

"Thank you for letting me inhabit your body. It is now time to exit," I say.

Again, nothing.

"I really don't think it's good to isolate in Molly's room," my mother says.

"You're definitely right," I say. "I'm coming."

But I'm stuck. Inside Sadie. Inside my own sadness. My soul must be cursed. Or maybe all souls are cursed. I turn this idea over a few times in my head as I consider how complicated it is to actually possess your friend. Then an idea strikes me. Maybe I need to return Sadie to the position I found her in when I possessed her. I fall to the floor and reach under my bed. Then I will myself to peel out of her. "Separate. Separate. Separate," I chant. And it works. I speed away from Sadie's body with such force that I'm dazed. My mother opens the door and Sadie is on the floor.

"Are you okay?" my mother asks. "Are you praying?"

Sadie looks beyond confused. This is so hard to watch. She crawls out from under my bed and sits on my floor.

"Whoa," she says.

"I know," my mother says. "Grief hits me in waves too."

"Yeah," Sadie says. She reaches down and touches her thighs. "I feel weird."

"I know exactly what you mean," my mother says. "Why don't you get your things and join us in the living room. And don't forget your shoes."

Sadie wobbles to her feet and takes hold of my desk chair to support herself. She looks like she doesn't know where she is, but my mother doesn't seem to notice. She's attributing everything to some sort of grief tsunami. After my mother leaves, Sadie wanders to the window and looks for Henry. But he's gone. Then she walks to my desk and sees what I wrote.

"How come I didn't notice this before? You wanted to ask Henry to the Sweetheart Ball?" Sadie says. "No. He has a girlfriend. You made the same mistake at the Thirsty Truck. You mean Tate." She leaves the note on my dresser next to a blush brush.

Then she reads the part about her ring. She stares at the note. "When did you write this?" She looks closer. "It looks like my handwriting." I watch goose pimples rise on her skin. "I feel so creeped out right now."

Sadie lets the note flutter to the floor. She looks like she's afraid of it. I guess that makes sense. It would be weird to read your own handwriting on a note you never wrote.

"I'm sorry," I say.

Sadie grabs her backpack and runs out of my room. In the living room, my mother stands in front of Tate, holding the pint of ice cream for him to take. "Molly really wanted to ask you to the Sweetheart Ball," she says. "She was going to take this ice cream."

"I, uh, don't know what to say," Tate stammers.

Of course he doesn't know what to say. It's completely weird for a dead girl's mother to invite a guy to a dance on her daughter's behalf using a dairy product. Don't do it. Leave things as they are. Watching my mother push the pint toward Tate makes me feel incredibly anxious. Could inviting the wrong guy to a girls'-choice dance injure my lasting connection to the right guy? It seems like it could.

"You don't have to say anything," my mother says. "Just take it."

I watch Tate reach out and accept the ice cream. I can tell by the way he holds it that he's not sure whether he wants it. We weren't in love. The invitation must feel like a burden.

Right now, in my driveway, the boy I really love sits in a car holding a bag of items I stole. And my funeral is tomorrow. I should feel like everything is over, but I don't. Because what just happened in my bedroom has changed everything. If I stay, if I don't cross, if I maintain a connection to my life, with Hilda's help I may be able to find a different way to live.

twenty-two

Being dead is a lot of work. Especially when you're in the middle of a fight with your soul's intake counselor. Deep down, I know it was rude and inappropriate to command Louise to leave, but I don't think it was a mistake. Possessing Sadie accomplished many things, and I needed Louise gone in order to do that.

I arrive at the clock room to find the door shut. I'm standing in the hallway that I walked down with all the photographs of my life. The pictures are all gone. They should save the trip down memory lane for right before your funeral. Making you take it immediately after you die is a bad idea, because you're in so much shock that you miss a lot. Your life flashes by so rapidly that it's hard to engage with all your memories. It feels like it's over before it begins.

"Louise?" I call. "Louise?"

"I'm in my office," she answers from inside the room.

I look at the door. It would be impolite to just travel through it. "Can I come in?" I ask.

"Sure," she says.

The tone of her voice is completely flat. She hates me. I commanded her to leave and now she wants nothing to do with me. Fine. That's fine. I don't need her guidance anymore. I've got Hilda. And a few ideas of my own about how things should work. I try to travel through the door, but I can't move beyond the hallway. I try again. And again. It's as if I'm hitting a wall. Is this some sort of trick? If Louise doesn't want me to visit, why doesn't she just say that?

"I'm stuck," I say. "I can't get inside."

"If you want to get inside, you can get inside," she says in an I-don't-care-about-your-fate-anymore voice.

I push again. I try to make my foot enter the door, but it won't. I attempt another time, with my shoulder. I get so frustrated that I slam my head forward. But there's this gentle pressure, like a magnet opposing another magnet, keeping me from entering.

"The door is broken," I say.

"The door is not broken," Louise says.

I stretch my arms out in front of me to force my way in. Oh my god. Being stuck in the hallway is the least of my problems. I'm starting to glow. Why am I starting to glow?

"Something is happening to me," I say, with a fair amount of urgency and dread. "I think it's bad. I'm glowing."

Then I'm not alone anymore. I'm standing next to Louise. She's joined me in the hallway. "It's quite normal for your soul to become illuminated as your funeral approaches. As you cross, a powerful light will fire through you and deliver you to your next phase."

"I'm going to turn into a light?" I ask. This is one more reason not to cross.

"Molly, has anybody ever told you that you worry about all the wrong things?" Louise says.

I don't want to have any additional fights with Louise. So I only mildly defend myself.

"I'm concerned that I'm stuck in a hallway and also becoming translucent. Those feel like legitimate issues to worry about."

Louise looks so bored with me. "You still have one more moment to relive."

"Yeah," I say. My mind lands on the Henry kiss. Shouldn't I just relive that one again? I loved kissing Henry.

"Reliving the same moment twice is a bad idea," Louise says. "The whole reasoning behind the life moments is that you will gain new perspectives that you can take with you."

"So nobody cares anymore whether or not I'm having a good time? I die and all my happiness gets snuffed out?" I look down at my legs. Whoa. They are whiter than my arms. "I'm turning into some sort of awful glitter being."

"You've officially worn me down, Molly. Go relive whatever you want to relive. Did you eat a really good piece of pizza once? Track that down. You went to SeaWorld when you were younger, right? Go there again. Maybe you can re-watch the whale act."

"There's no need to be condescending," I say. "I'm a dead teenager. I'm not asking for all your sympathy. But maybe just a bit more."

"Fine, you're a dead teenager. And you are always going

to be a dead teenager. Forever. But guess what? I'm a dead mother. I'm a dead daughter. I'm a dead dancer. I'm a dead sister. I'm a dead woman, Molly Weller. And I have plenty of sympathy for you. The question is, do you have any for me? Are you able to get outside of yourself long enough to care about the fate of anybody but yourself?"

I stare at her. She's trying to make me feel terrible, and it's working. I know she used to be alive too. But she's had so much more time to get used to it. She's adjusted to being dead. I'm still wrapping my mind around it.

"I know you're a good person, Molly, but you don't challenge yourself enough. You're very stuck."

"I don't know if that's true."

"You are literally stuck in this hallway. No soul I've ever worked with has gotten stuck in the hallway."

I look around, first at my glowing body and then at the narrow walls of the space where I'm standing. Louise is right: I do feel stuck. I don't want to move forward. I don't want to accept my fate. Every impulse inside of me is to go back to my life. To return to the people who love me. But I don't get that option.

"I'm ready to relive my last life moment," I say.

"SeaWorld? Or pizza?" Louise says with a yawn.

I shake my head. "Something that matters."

I'm surprised when I hear myself say these words. Because I don't exactly know what I'll relive.

Louise looks directly at me and nods. Her face looks incredibly serious. "Everything you learn, you get to take with you, Molly."

I hope she's right. I let my mind begin to play possible scenes I could relive, but I'm still not sure. I find myself wanting to stall for more time. "You really didn't relive any life moments?" I ask.

She shakes her head. "No. It was a mistake. I should have."

"You just stayed next to your body?"

"I couldn't leave it," she explains.

That's not the experience I had when I saw my body at all. Maybe this is because Louise was more connected to hers. She was a dancer, so her body was her instrument. And she'd had her body longer than I had mine. I ask a question I've wanted to ask for a while. "How old were you when you died?"

"Thirty-four."

I imagine a child losing a mother. A sister losing a sister. A mother losing her daughter. "That's wrong."

She shrugs. "I've accepted it."

Now comes the other question I've been holding on to since the moment I learned Louise had once been alive. "How did you die?"

"You don't have time for this," Louise says.

"I do. Please tell me." Suddenly, how life was extinguished from my spirit guide matters a lot to me.

"I died in a fire," she's says. "At a hotel. I was on my final tour with my dance company."

I cover my mouth. This is horrific.

"A lot of us died that night," she says. "But tragedies happen every day."

"And they shouldn't!" I say. Shouldn't somebody be doing something about this? How can a bunch of dancers get killed in a hotel fire? That's rotten. Absolutely rotten. That shouldn't happen. Not only do I want to reject my death outright and be alive again, I want this for Louise too. I want her to be a not-dead mother, a not-dead dancer, a not-dead daughter, a not-dead sister. I'm not saying we should be immortal, but I wish we were given a little more time.

"Don't backslide. You've picked your moment to relive. Now, move into that moment."

Louise is right. I need to do this. I think of my moment with Henry and how I was guided to a place where I began to fall in love. There must be a starting point like that for other things. Worse things. I need to go there and confront what it is about myself that I don't want to see.

"I steal and I don't understand why. It's got to come from somewhere. Take me to where it started."

Before I can think another thought, I am in a tunnel and then I am slamming into the world again. I'm a child. Maybe four years old. And I'm with my grandmother. She is so cautious. So anxious. My grandfather must have just recently died, because I see a picture of him taped to the dashboard. I can remember my mother telling me that my grandma did this shortly after the funeral. It stayed there for a year, until one day on a road trip to Arizona, a gust of wind swept through and blew the picture into a gorge.

"You have his chin," Grandma tells me. "A perfect profile."

"Yeah," I say. "Grandpa's chin." I feel myself touching my chin with my finger. This must be a game we've played before. My grandma looks very amused.

"Why don't you wait in the car while I mail these?" She waves a handful of envelopes at me.

I fidget with the seat belt. I want to go inside. I'm a kid. I don't want to sit inside a car on a hot day.

"Can I come?" I ask, kicking with my legs. I'm sitting buckled into a car seat in back.

"You'd better wait here." She takes the keys out of the ignition and sets them on the passenger seat. And gets out. I keep kicking with my legs. In this moment, I am young and bored and carefree. With the air conditioner off, I'm able to feel the tremendous heat of the day starting to press itself through the windows. There's a small Baggie full of cereal next to me, and I pick it up. I lick my fingertip and touch a puffed-oat piece and then carefully place it in my mouth. *Crunch.* Through the window, I see my grandma rushing to the mailbox outside the post office. She's wearing a light blue pantsuit and the whitest sneakers money will buy. Years later, my mother will tell me about all the errands I helped my grandma run following my grandpa's death. Apparently, she liked to drive around and tell me stories about him. But I can't remember him. He feels like a stranger to me now.

Then it happens. My grandma realizes that she's locked her keys in the car. And I'm stuck in here. My fingers are wet with slobber. I can't get the door to unlock. I drop the Baggie, and cereal explodes onto the floor. I use my fingers to press the release button on the seat belt, but it's old and clunky and won't budge. I keep trying.

"Open the door, Molly. You can do it," my grandma calls. Her voice gets louder.

But I can't do it. I jam my fingers into the metal square. Trying. Trying. But it won't click open.

"Help me," I say. I feel the adrenaline really starting to flow.

My grandma becomes frantic. "Help us! Help us!" she cries. Within two minutes, a small group of people has gathered. One is a postal employee with a thick beard. He lowers his face to the backseat window on the driver's side.

"Can you open the door?" he coos. "Can you press the button and let us inside?"

But there isn't a button. There are thin knobs on top of the door that I can't pull up. "I'm stuck!" I say, getting more and more scared.

"We should call the police," a woman says. "It's too hot in there."

I am sobbing in the backseat now. I gasp for air and shudder. My fears are uncontrollable. I want out. I worry that I may die inside the car. I worry that it's so hot that I might melt, even though my grandma is standing right there, just outside the car.

"Don't cry," my grandma says. "The police are coming."

I hear the sirens. Blue-and-red lights pulse in the background. Then there is a policeman standing next to my grandma.

"She can't unlock it?" the policeman asks.

"She's tried," my grandma says.

I keep pressing on the buckle. It's getting hotter, and my fingers feel more slippery. I'm sweating. I see the man insert something into the door, but nothing happens. He tries again. And again. I am screaming now.

"We need to break a front window," the policeman says. "Keep her attention in the backseat."

I don't want them to break a window. Even at four, I'm afraid the glass will shatter on me and cut me. "No! No!" I say. I try harder to make the buckle pop open.

"When we get done here we'll go get a delicious lunch," my grandma says.

I'm not hungry. I don't care. I feel like I'm dying.

"Help!" I say. I keep pushing on the lock. It won't open, and I can't stay trapped here. I decide to try a different door. The policeman has pulled his arm back to punch something through the window. He doesn't see me as I scamper into the front seat to unlock the door. He makes impact with the window, and tiny pieces of glass shower onto me. They cut my bare legs. They scrape across my arms and leave bloody lines.

"Oh my god!" my grandmother screams.

I'm screaming too. I've fallen into the passenger seat on top of the pebbled glass. I feel the sharp edges bite into my skin. Then a stranger's hands pull me through the opened door.

"You're okay," the policeman says.

I do not feel okay.

Grandma races up and holds me so tightly that her shirt

gets smeared with my blood. "We'll take you home. And clean you up. And take you to the store and you can get anything you like."

I am sobbing so hard I begin to convulse.

"You're fine. You're fine," Grandma says as she holds me.

I am not fine.

"You should take her to the doctor," the policeman says. "She's got a lot of cuts."

"No!" I scream. I want to go home. I don't want the experience to last any longer. I screw my eyes closed and gasp for breath.

"Here you go," a woman says. She presses something soft into my hands. I open my eyes. It's a toy. It's a stuffed bear. "I bought it for my own granddaughter just now. But you can take it."

And somehow holding this soft new thing that was intended for somebody else lets my anxiety flow out of me. I'm not trapped anymore. I'm out. I'm not going to melt to death. Glass isn't going to cut me to ribbons. My breathing slows. I hold the bear.

"That's a good girl," my grandma says. Then she turns to the woman who gave me the toy. "I need to call my daughter."

The woman hands my grandmother her phone. I keep holding the bear. When we get home, my mother decides not to take me to the doctor. She calls a friend who's a nurse and they pick the glass out of my skin with tweezers and apply alcohol to sterilize my cuts. All I will need is a few Band-Aids. But my stuffed bear will be taken from me.

The toy, spotted with blood, and given to me by a stranger, will vanish that night. My mother will toss it in the trash while I sleep and offer me a different toy the next day. But it won't be enough. That sense of panic and loss will dwell within me for the rest of my life.

"You're okay," my grandma repeats as she sets me down on the sidewalk. The heat of the day is fading. My scrapes are losing their zing of pain. My last memory is ending. I don't quite feel that I've confronted anything. The moment traumatized me. I never got over it. The feelings I had inside that car are incredibly familiar. They are the same anxieties that ricochet through me before I steal. That's why I do it. I started stealing things in an effort to calm my escalating anxiety.

If I'd lived, maybe even just a year longer, I bet I would have told somebody about my problem. Maybe Henry. I imagine a therapist would have helped me develop other strategies. And maybe just telling people would have cured some of it too. While alive, I was so hard on myself for taking things. *Too hard.* Even here I've been pretty scared about what it means to be a thief and to be dead. But it's not like the people who love me would suddenly stop if they found out. Sadie didn't. Henry didn't. That's not what will damage my connections. And it's not going to determine what happens to me here, either. I'm not going to be shipped off to some terrible place and punished forever. Anxiety issues don't determine what happens to a soul. The fact that I was a kleptomaniac doesn't have anything to do with my fate now.

twenty-three

I don't return to Louise or the transition room. Yes, I've had a big breakthrough, and I look forward to telling her about it eventually. But there's also that matter of recently possessing Sadie. Taking over a body just sounds bad. Telling Louise about that incident feels like it would be a huge mistake. So I decide to do something else.

I arrive at my body's side. Before, when I stood next to it, I felt like I was dying all over again. Having to confront my pale, stiff corpse was too much. But I don't feel that way now. I am just here, and I watch as my grandma and Aunt Claire apply the last of my makeup. It's a relief to see that they're doing it right. I was afraid they'd make me look fake, like a doll. But I almost look like me. Almost.

"Less is more," Aunt Claire says, dotting my cheek with a light blush.

"I don't know how we'll go on," Grandma says.

They stand in silence, looking down at me. That's when I realize that I'm wearing my burial clothes. It's my green dress. I knew they'd make me look too formal. I only wore that outfit once, to a luncheon with my mother at a fancy hotel. Jeans would have made more sense. And a nice casual top. That was who I was. Why did I ever buy this green dress? It's the color of a pine tree. I stare at my dressed-up body and feel as though I'm about to enter a grief trance. I could stand here and feel sad for the rest of my existence. And I suspect I'd feel that way no matter what I was wearing.

"When you die in high school, wherever you go afterward, I bet you feel completely robbed. Like your whole life got stolen." My grandma tries to restrain her emotion when she speaks, and it makes her voice shake. "It's different when old people die. We lived. But Molly . . . There was so much ahead of her."

"I found something in her room," Aunt Claire says guiltily. "Remember when we grabbed the garment bag and I forgot the blush brush and I had to double back for it?"

My grandma dabs at her nose with a tissue. "Yes? What did you find?"

"A note."

It must have been the note I wrote when I was inside Sadie.

"It was about a boy," Aunt Claire says.

Grandma sniffles. "That sounds right. I think Molly might have been falling in love."

"With Henry?" Aunt Claire asks.

My whole soul feels alive with electricity. I'm not the only one who knows. And Henry's not the only one who knows. Other people now know that we were falling in love. Why does this make me feel relieved instead of doomed?

"What does the note say?" my grandma asks.

"She says she wants to ask him to the Sweetheart Ball," Aunt Claire says.

My grandmother starts sobbing. "She's missing prom. She's missing high school. She's missing her whole life."

"Shh," Aunt Claire says. "I know. I almost didn't say anything. But I wonder whether or not we should tell him."

My grandma nods. "Of course we should. Right?"

Aunt Claire smiles. "Her mother said Molly had planned on asking her date out with a pint of ice cream."

"Should we give it to him?" my grandma asks.

"Nice idea," I say. "But it's too late. Mom already gave it to Tate."

But then I remember that I bought two pints. Why not invite both guys? So Henry will get not only the note from Sadie, he'll also get the ice-cream invitation. Maybe it will help him understand that we had something real. Something that was going somewhere. Because my note tells him that.

They walk toward the exit, and both of them look back at me. "So we just bum-rush the boy at the funeral with a pint of ice cream and tell him that Molly wanted to ask him to the prom?" my grandma says.

"When you say it that way, it sounds like a bad idea," Aunt Claire says.

"Well, I don't want my grief to cloud my judgment," my grandma says.

I've grown attached to the idea of Henry's getting the ice

cream. It's the better option. "You should give it to him," I say.

"I think we're both having a hard time accepting that Molly's life is really over," Aunt Claire says.

My grandmother tears up again and nods. "Things happened the way they happened, and now we all have to live with them."

"Let's not invite him," Aunt Claire says.

This isn't right. It's like the world is conspiring against me and Henry. Like I was never meant to stay connected with him. I know what I need to do. Even though I've only done it one time and I'm still uncomfortable with the overall concept of it, I need to possess Aunt Claire and make her invite Henry to the dance for me. After you possess one person, I imagine that each subsequent possession only gets easier and easier. I mean, it really shouldn't be a problem. When I have my next meeting with Hilda, I'll need to ask her some questions about the logistics of possession. Clearly, there should be some sort of time limit. Like, I can't just stay and inhabit another person's body for an entire week, or even a day.

I move toward Aunt Claire and get ready to pounce on her. Then I reconsider. Maybe I should wait until she gets closer to Henry. That makes more sense. It would be too weird for my grandma if I possessed Aunt Claire and made them both drive to Henry's right now. I can't do that. Though I'm not sure how to predict when Aunt Claire will get closer to Henry. I should probably wait until my funeral. I hear a door slam. Aunt Claire has left. My chance to possess her is basically over.

I'm ready to leave when I realize that Ruthann is walking into the room that holds my body. This really shouldn't be allowed. Don't funeral homes have attendants to keep people from walking right in off the street? She approaches my casket cautiously, as if I might jump out from my cushioned box.

"Hi, Molly," she says, lamely waving at my casket. "You're probably wondering why I'm here." She's standing near my head, staring at my dead face.

"I came to say I'm sorry." She bites her lip and keeps looking at me like she thinks I'm going to respond. "You probably think it's crazy that I'm apologizing to you. But I'm not actually apologizing for anything I've done, because that wouldn't really make sense. This is a preemptive apology for something I'm going to do."

She sniffles a little and turns her back to me. Never in my life did I ever expect anybody to deliver a preemptive apology to me. Especially Ruthann Culpepper.

"I've developed feelings for somebody you care about. Real. Serious. Romantic feelings. And while a part of me thinks the honorable thing to do would be to shelve them and deny my heart what it wants, so I don't violate our awesome friendship, there is another part of me that thinks the right choice would be to act on these feelings."

Oh my god. If she tells me that she's going to pursue a romantic relationship with Henry, I'm going to have to figure out a way to possess somebody who has the means and equipment to lock Ruthann Culpepper in a box. Forever.

"I think you probably saw the chemistry already between me and Tate. And I think if everybody involved could just be honest with each other, the real reason he fired me probably had more to do with all our sexual tension than with any other excuse he gave."

She really is crazy. For the first time since my accident, I'm sort of glad I'm dead so I don't actually have to respond to her during this awkward confession. "There is no way you and Tate had sexual chemistry," I say. "Zero possibility."

Ruthann reaches out and places a hand on my casket. I don't like watching her invade my body's space. She needs to stand back. "So I'm hoping you will give me your blessing. And I'm just going to stand here for a second until I feel like you've delivered that."

And so she just stands there. Next to my body. At the funeral home. Waiting for some sort of sign that is never going to appear. This is nuts. So I tell her. Except I don't use those exact words.

"You don't need my permission to explore something with Tate. I mean, he's going to reject you, because he's repulsed by you. But you don't need my blessing. Tate and I didn't really have anything. Things wouldn't have gone much further than the first date, had I lived."

"Thanks," Ruthann says. "I totally think I just felt you give me your permission."

"This is classic," I say. "You hear me as well in death as you did in life."

Ruthann exhales dramatically and keeps talking. "And also, I wanted to let you know that I'm not pursuing any charges against your cat. My mom and I think it wouldn't be the right thing to do under these circumstances."

This is great news, but it's odd that Ruthann is standing over my dead body to deliver it.

"So, I think we're done here," Ruthann says. "Bye, Molly." She pulls her hand away from my casket and waves. Then she walks out. I could follow her to see where she's going, but I don't really want to do that. It's over. I need to let Ruthann leave. I need to let her go off and live her ridiculous life.

After she goes, I stand by my body. Partly because there is this comfortable hold that it has on my soul. Partly because it's one of the last times I'm going to see it. Louise told me that my friends and family would heal and go on, and it looks like that's already starting to happen. I'm not even buried and people are planning the shape they want their lives to take without me.

twenty-four

$\mathcal{E}$verything feels wrong now. It's the morning of my funeral, and I know I promised Hilda that I'd meet her so she could teach me how to remain uncrossed, but I'm beginning to have serious doubts about that plan.

"I'm miserable," I say as I approach the snow cone stand. But that's probably typical. I bet most people feel this way on the day of their funeral, especially when they're young, like me, and have lost everything. *Everything.* I'm not sure being uncrossed is going to make my situation better. The more I think about it, the more I start to see the obvious flaws. So I'll just stay here and watch everybody I love grow older and older. Until they eventually die. Then what happens? I just keep staying here? If I refuse to cross now, does that mean that I never cross?

I'm inside the hut now, and it's just as Hilda and I left it. Straws and napkins scattered on the floor. Sticky flavorings drip down the sides of the bottles. I try to shake off a feeling of depression. Because this isn't where I'd stay. I'd

240

hang out in my bedroom. The hallways at school. Until my friends graduated. It would be weird to keep hanging out in high school when I didn't know anybody. I'd get to see the seasons change. See my family buy groceries and eat dinner. Attend the twins' birthday parties.

But I wouldn't feel any of it. It would be like going to an aquarium. Lots of interesting things would be happening, but I'd always be stuck on the other side of the glass. What's the longest I've ever stared at an aquarium, anyway?

"I'm here, Hilda." I'm still trying to avoid thinking or saying things in the form of a question. I don't want Louise to know what I'm considering. "Hilda," I yell. It's rude for her to be late. I'm running on a pretty tight timeline. If I do it, I'll be crossing over in just a few hours.

As crazy as it seems, I'm starting to feel like I should just cross. It's part of death. The hardest part is not knowing what's going to happen to me.

I see Hilda, and I voice my concerns right away. "I just don't want to be the sort of ghost who never goes any-where, who never advances into anything else."

"Being a ghost is a form of advancement," Hilda offers.

"Right," I say. "But I don't want to be stuck in this place where everybody else is living and feeling and getting on with their lives and I remain in my bedroom, unchanged."

"That's death, Molly," Hilda says.

"No," I say. "That's something else. Something stagnant. I'd feel creepy tailing everybody I loved. What? I'm going to watch Henry fall in love with somebody else? That would be terrible."

"Maybe you could interfere and prevent him from falling in love with somebody else."

That sounds appealing. For two seconds.

"No," I say. "That's terrible in a different way."

"Molly, stop doubting yourself," Hilda says. "Today I'm going to take you to a park and teach you how to possess a stranger. It's going to be harder than possessing Sadie. But I'm certain you can do it."

"Possess a stranger?" I'm horrified. That's not who I am. I don't want to be the kind of person who races around on the day of my funeral jumping into strange people's bodies.

"You really have a gift for it," Hilda says. "Not every-body can inhabit a body as effortlessly as you did and make it function properly."

I can't handle hearing any more compliments about my innate skills for possessing people. The more I reflect on it, the more I'm ashamed that I did it in the first place.

"Hilda," I say, "I want to learn this stuff. But at the same time, I don't want to learn this stuff. It feels unnatural. I really don't think I can go along with it."

"Let's go down to the river," Hilda says. "I'll let you choose the person."

When she puts it to me that way, it's clear that I abso-lutely cannot do this.

My funeral is in a matter of hours. I should be comfort-ing people. I shouldn't be violating the laws of souldom.

"Just follow me," Hilda says.

And I'm not sure why I do. I guess I want her to under-stand why I'm backing out. Plus, I hate disappointing people.

"At this point, it just doesn't feel like the path I should take," I say as we approach the bridge.

Hilda refuses to stop.

"Really," I say, "I don't see this second possession happening."

She keeps moving. And I keep moving. Because I want her at least to acknowledge that I've completely backed out.

"Just give it one try," she says.

I slow my pace. Hilda needs to accept my decision. Because I'm not going to make the same mistakes in death that I made in life. While alive, I was way too much of a follower. Now that I'm dead, I'm planning to be a little more proactive.

"Hilda, you don't seem to be listening. I'm not going to do it," I say. "It feels wrong."

Hilda's anger travels through the air and lands on me; it's the closest thing to heat that I've encountered since I died. It's time to get out of this. For real.

"I appreciate everything you've done," I say, "but I need to go."

She ignores me and picks up a small mallard. Then she turns to me and her face is wild with rage.

"You led me to believe you would do this," she says. "You're a liar."

"I don't think I lied. I thought I could do this, but now I don't think I can anymore."

"Look at what you're doing. Look at how you're treating me."

Her grip on the duck is so tight that the bird lets out a quack.

"Why are you holding that duck like that?" I ask.

"To show you what you're missing," she says. "I can touch anything. Move any object. And if I feel like it, I can possess any body I want. You could have this too."

"Right," I say, taking a few steps back.

Her reaction seems severe. I just met her and she's acting like a jilted lover. Like she'd pinned her whole future on teaching me how to possess somebody.

"Calm down," I tell her. But based on her glare, I guess that our conversation is having the opposite effect. I don't know why she's acting this way. All I can think is that she must be lonely. She must have figured we were going to become friends and spend hours and hours of soul time together. I'd become her apprentice and we'd navigate the uncrossed place together. Sure, she's probably disappointed, but it's not like I made a promise to her.

"I'm going to cross," I explain. "You shouldn't take it personally."

I look around beneath the bridge as the river slips quietly by.

"Your family will go on without you," she says.

"They'll move on either way," I reply. "I'm dead. I matter in a different way to them."

Just as with Sadie, I can feel Hilda aiming her anger at me. I take a step back, and then another. She slowly sets down the duck and it flies toward the water.

"I should probably be going," I say.

"You're making a mistake," she says.

I shrug. "I've made a lot of those. And this doesn't feel like one of them. It feels like the right thing to do."

She shakes her head. "Why did you even come here?"

"I guess I wanted to tell you face to face," I say, truly trying to let her down easy.

She smiles. "You have doubts. That's why you're here."

And I do have doubts. But I'm not going to admit that to Hilda.

"No," I say. "I've made my decision."

"Well, you'll have a lot of years to live with it."

Hilda walks under the bridge, but before she gets too far, she turns and says, "You're going to be miserable."

"Maybe," I say. "But maybe not."

She glares at me. Then she smiles a very creepy smile and says something that's confusing and unsettling.

"You'll only cross if I let you."

Then she's gone, and I want to believe it's for good. But her threat makes it very clear that she's not done with me yet.

twenty-five

'm going to have to tell Louise what I've done. Everything. I can't leave anything out. Because when you've been threatened by a menacing uncrossed soul, really the best (and only) place to turn for help is the intake counselor of your soul. I'm not sure why it takes several attempts to make a tunnel appear again, but it does. And when it finally arrives, things seem to move much slower than normal. Usually I enter and rush to where I'm headed at the speed of thought. Not this time.

Just like before, I arrive in the hallway instead of the actual transition room. Louise stands waiting, presumably for me.

"Where have you been?" she asks.

I've got hours before my funeral, so I don't understand why she's so upset. And I also don't want to tell her where I've been.

"What's wrong?" I ask.

"What did you do?" she asks.

I thought I would ease into telling Louise about what

I'd done. I'm not sure how to start confessing things. Fortunately, it looks like I don't have time to do that right now anyway.

"Something has happened. You only have twelve clocks left," she says. "And your funeral is about to start. Why are you late?"

I don't know why I'm late and I can hardly process what she's saying. "Twelve clocks! Is Henry still there? My parents? My grandma?" Maybe it's okay that I only have twelve clocks left.

"Didn't you hear me?" Louise says. "Your funeral is about to start."

She grabs my soul and makes a tunnel, and just like that I am swooped to my funeral. Where did the time go? Hilda. She must have done something, but I don't know exactly what.

I walk into the mortuary and see my friends and family gathered in the cushioned pews. My body is at center stage.

"Has it just started?" I ask.

Louise nods. She looks concerned. Why should she be so concerned? I'm the one with only twelve lousy clocks.

I spot my parents seated in the front row, next to Aunt Claire and my grandmother. I don't see Henry. Did he not come? Tate and Sadie are sitting with Joy and Roy Ekles. Wow. Joy and Roy make a great couple. I wonder if my death helped motivate her to get that relationship off the ground. If the shoe were on the other foot, I bet one of my friends' deaths would have affected me that same way. If there was something I wanted to do, I'd do it. If there was somebody I liked, I'd make my move. I'm happy for her. I really am. Then I start looking around for Henry.

But Ruthann Culpepper is here. She doesn't look as sad as when she came and spoke to me at the funeral home. She looks pretty happy. And she's not wearing black. She's wearing a brown skirt with a tangerine blouse, short-sleeved, of course. How else could everyone see her scratches? She hasn't come with her parents. She walks over to Joy and smiles.

"This is so heavy," Ruthann says. "Hey. Have you seen Tate?"

I keep scouting around for Henry. I even leave the room. He's not in the bathroom. I leave the building. He's not in the parking lot. Where is he? Do I not matter to him?

I return to the room, and a group of parents are descending upon my grieving family.

"The flowers are lovely," a woman says.

"Thank you," my grandma says.

"We're very sorry for your loss," she says.

My grandma chokes back some tears and takes a deep breath. It looks like her mind is spinning. I bet she's thinking about Grandpa Jean.

"Her sweet spirit is in a far better place," a random person leans down to tell Aunt Claire. *Gross.* What's that supposed to mean? My sweet spirit is right here.

I glance at my body and notice a large arrangement of flowers hanging on an easel. A banner that reads OUR BELOVED DAUGHTER is draped across it. Who ordered that?

"This is the saddest day of my life," I say.

"It's supposed to be," Louise says. "It's the last time you'll be connected to these people in this way."

"Louise, what's going to happen to me? I don't want to be all alone."

"It's different for everyone, Molly," Louise says. "I've already told you that there isn't anything more I can offer."

"But I saw a dead man and his wife together. I mean, I saw their souls. I think she helped him cross. Maybe I'll get that. Maybe you can go with me and help me."

"They were life partners and were headed for the same destination. It was prearranged. You don't have a life partner."

"No, I don't." All I can do is think of Henry.

"This is what I know. During the service, toward the end, you'll be presented with a door. You'll move toward it, and you'll be pulled through as if by a breeze."

Really, I think. I think I've seen a commercial for a dryer sheet that is a lot like that. A woman walks to an open set of French doors, takes a deep breath, and is sucked out into a meadow.

"Then you'll progress," she says.

"Okay," I say.

"Whatever happens, I assure you that you're going to be okay," Louise says.

But Louise doesn't know what I've done. I need to tell her about Hilda. Because when she told me that I would only cross if she let me, I don't think she was lying. Her threat felt genuine.

"Louise, please don't get mad at me, but I need to tell

you something." *How do I phrase this?* "You're not the only soul who has been helping me." I look at Louise and smile, trying to pass this off like it's not a big deal. But Louise's face radiates concern.

"Molly, you didn't."

I shrug. "I don't know. I might have," I say.

"Molly Weller, you did not invite an uncrossed soul into your life."

"No, I didn't."

"Then what soul have you been talking to?"

"Well, I invited an uncrossed soul into my *after*life."

Louise buries her head in her hands. I think she's crying.

"It can't be that big a deal. I've decided to cross. I'm not going to listen to her. I never even learned how to possess the body of a stranger. It's okay. I'm on track."

"Molly, it's not that easy. You've committed a grave error. Did you let her teach you anything?"

My mind flashes back to possessing Sadie. I don't want to admit that I did that. "Louise, you never even told me about uncrossed souls."

"I tell a soul what it needs to know."

"That's not true!" I say. "You're hardly ever direct. I mean, I had to figure out a lot of stuff on my own."

"That's the point," Louise says. "You're supposed to strengthen yourself."

"Well, not only did I do that, but I also managed to clear my room of all that stolen stuff. And that seems important."

"Why would that be important? And how did you manage to do that?"

It's time to fess up. "I sort of possessed my friend Sadie."

"What?" Louise looks and sounds aghast. "Why would you do that to Sadie? You can't put somebody's soul in jeopardy like that."

"She's fine," I said. "I was able to write letters to my loved ones, which she's presumably distributing. It's working out really well."

"You possessed your friend and penned notes beyond the grave and you call that working out really well?" Louise wags her finger in my face. "When you possess somebody, you dislocate their soul. And the souls of the living are very fragile. Some don't make it back. Some get damaged. It's unnatural to force a soul from its home."

That makes sense. Hilda never told me that. "She's fine. And the letters are going to help everybody grieve. I didn't get a chance to say good-bye. I died too soon."

"It was your time! We've been through this."

"But if I'd had a later exit date I could have gotten more done. I would have said those things to people. I didn't really change anything. I fixed something. And I don't feel bad about that. I did die too young."

I wait for Louise to launch into an argument, but she doesn't. Judging by the look on her face, she seems to agree. "You died very young. I don't agree with what you did, but I understand it."

Upon hearing this, I start feeling so much better.

"Molly, we need to get back to a serious issue. I need to know where you invited the uncrossed soul into your life."

"I don't want to talk about it," I say. "I'm upset. Watching everybody I love grieve at my funeral makes me feel like I wasted my whole life."

"Molly!" Louise says. "This is important. Tell me how you invited the uncrossed soul into your life?"

"It just happened."

"When?" she demands.

"A couple of days ago," I say.

"Where?" she presses.

I point into the hallway, to a spot next to the water fountain. "Right about there."

"Here, in the funeral home?" Louise looks horrified.

"Yes," I say.

And then a saxophone begins to play. It's Henry. The sound coming from his horn makes my soul begin to glow. Brighter and brighter. Just like Louise said, I'm becoming light.

"I love him," I tell Louise. "I think we were meant to be together. How can I leave him?"

"Oh, Molly, this is more serious than I thought. You may not be going anywhere."

twenty-six

I can't explain what it feels like to see the first guy you love playing a saxophone at your funeral. It sucks and it's wonderful at the same time. And the song. Once I recognize it, the melody sweeps over me. It's enough to break my already broken heart. Henry is playing "I Remember Clifford." The song that was written for the trumpet player who was killed in that car crash. The sound escapes Henry's horn like a mournful cry. I am going to miss him. I am going to miss everyone.

My attention keeps getting split between Sadie and Henry. Why? There's something dragging my focus to her. That's when I notice the notes. People are holding pieces of paper. My grandma, Ruthann, Aunt Claire. Sadie already handed them out. That means that Henry has his note too. I am so relieved. She is such a good friend.

Before Henry finishes playing, Louise leans down and tells me, "Molly, I've got to leave now. I can't be in the room when you cross."

"Wait. So I will be crossing?" I ask. "You made it sound like I wouldn't be."

I want to focus on Henry's song; I want to watch the looks on people's faces as they read their notes. So much is happening.

"Molly, soon you are going to be presented with a door."

Every word Louise says feels important. But I can't stop myself from interrupting her. "Will I see my parents again? Will I get to fall in love with Henry and actually be able to be with him?"

The music is over. I've missed almost all of it.

"I can't answer those questions," Louise says. "You'll need to cross and find your way. You'll need to go through your door."

I nod. I sense that I'm teetering on the brink of finality. Everything is going to change in a matter of minutes.

"Molly, because of your mistake, you won't be alone. The uncrossed soul will be in the room with you. They tend to hide, disguised as mourners."

"Well, that's stupid. I'll know all the mourners."

"You won't be able to recognize the uncrossed soul. When the door appears, the soul will try to beat you to the portal. If it gets there first, you won't be crossing."

"Shut up. It's like a race? That's so arbitrary."

"You made it that way."

"Where in the room do the portals appear?"

"It's always different."

"At what point in the funeral will it arrive?"

"It varies with each service."

"I thought you said it was toward the end."

"That's when it didn't matter. I wanted you to sit back and enjoy what people had to say. I didn't want you to be stressed out about looking for the door."

"But now you want me to be stressed out?"

"Molly, be alert. You've got to get there first."

Louise is fading away.

"Don't go. I feel so overwhelmed. So unsure."

Joy bursts into tears. She's reading my note. What did I write? I thought it was nice. I move closer to her and look at it.

Joy,
You are a great friend. Forget our fight
at the mall; it doesn't matter. You know what matters:
this quote by Mae West: "You only live once,
but if you do it right, once is enough."
Friends forever!
Love, Molly

"She was so funny," Joy whispers.

Sadie hugs her.

And now my funeral is really under way. I hear my father say, "It's time to close the casket."

I thought my casket would be left open for the service. But that's not the case. I watch as the funeral worker lowers the lid. That's it. My body will never see light again.

255

My parents commence sobbing, and it's likely the last time I'll witness it. Another funeral worker stands to the side of my casket, with his hands clasped over his fly. I think it's his default position.

"I can't imagine our lives without her," my father says.

My mother rubs his back. "Stop," she says. "We can't fall apart."

"I think she'd want me to be this sad," my father says.

My mother nods.

But I can't keep my attention focused solely on them. I need to find Hilda. Why did I even invite her to appear? At first, I try to blame Louise. If only she had told me what to do. But then I realize I'm all wrong. I should have been smart enough to know what to do. I should have thought about it. I should have considered the risks. This is my fault. I did a stupid thing. I'm the one who has to correct it.

I bet Hilda can run pretty fast. I wonder whether, if we both arrive at the door at the same exact time, I'll have to fight another soul. I don't want to wrestle Hilda for my spot in the afterlife. How would two souls even do that? We're both basically like air. Is Hilda going to be able to punch me? Will I be able to pull her hair? Can a soul put another soul in a sleeper hold?

Maybe Hilda can morph her face and look like someone else. Or maybe she can morph her entire body. I'm suddenly drawn to investigate a conspicuous rubber-tree plant propped in the corner.

Organ music begins.

My attention is pulled to Ruthann. She's reading the note I wrote her.

I don't know what you've lost in life, or who has hurt you, but it's clear to me that you take your pain out on others. I wish you could see that acting the way you do is a choice. We all have choices. You know, you could choose to be a better person. . . .

She doesn't appear to finish reading the note and rips the paper into tiny pieces.

"She never knew me that well," she mumbles. "What kind of person writes a note like this and dies?"

Some of the pieces tumble to the floor. It's going to take a lot to change Ruthann Culpepper from the person she is to the person she could be. I hope she can handle what life throws her way.

At this moment, I feel certain about who I was. As people read the notes, Molly Weller's true self is revealed. Not just to them, but to me too. I understand myself. I wasn't just a bad friend. Or a kleptomaniac. Or a high school junior hung up on becoming popular.

The last years of my life were not a cakewalk. I wasn't moving effortlessly from point A to point B. Mine was a stressful existence. But I was surviving. To live inside your imperfect skin and consistently find ways to deal with pain and disappointment is no easy task. But I wasn't a failure. I see that now. Not only do I feel like I know who I was, I feel like I know where I'm going.

Wait. I'm wrong. I have no idea where I'm going. If I go through the door, where will I arrive when I cross? I'm scanning the faces of all the people. Hilda could easily be passing herself off as a parent of one of my classmates. I don't know what everybody's freaking parent looks like.

Where will I go? Seriously, *where will I go?*

I catch Aunt Claire reading her note. She's in the front row.

You are wonderful and I love you. Because of you and your stories I always wanted to visit every county in Ireland. And take out the maximum level of insurance on my rental car. Who knew it would be the driver's fault if a tour bus sideswiped you on a mountain pass near Kenmare and ripped off your side mirror and back bumper?

My aunt weeps over the fact that I'll never eat fish and chips at a café in Kinsale, or kiss the Blarney Stone in County Cork.

My grandma is preoccupied by her own note.

Thanks for teaching me how to make apple dumplings. I never thought that that recipe would help me land a catch half as good as Grandpa.

She dabs at the corners of her eyes with a tissue. She looks around like she's wondering whether or not my grandpa is here. I don't think he is. I've never met him. He died before I was born, but I get the sense that he moved on and is now in the middle of doing something important.

Ruthann looks very alone. She's sitting next to Mr. Dunkley, my fifth grade teacher, and his gray-haired wife, but that only makes her appear more isolated. Sort of like a loser. But I guess I shouldn't judge people. Especially at my funeral.

I take one last look at her. My torn note has fallen around her seat like snow. I have done all I can for her.

Vice Principal Oswald stands behind the white podium. Two large crystal vases of lilies flank both sides of her.

"I first met Molly Weller when she was in the third grade. I'd been invited to visit her elementary school as a judge for a science fair. I remember Molly because I remember her project. She created an ant race."

A few people in the crowd laugh. I barely remember this.

"She wanted to combine the ingenuity of the ant farm with the pizzazz of the rat maze. The outcome was the ant maze."

More light laughter.

"After hearing on the Discovery Channel that an ant colony had the greatest collection of intelligence on the planet—'Greater than that of man or the blue whale,' she pointed out—Molly wanted to see how quickly a gathering of ants could navigate a maze."

A lot more laughter.

"The prize she offered the successful ant was a piece of popcorn."

I'm not sure I like this speech. She's making me sound like an extremely dopey third grader.

"She kept the ants in a sandwich bag. Not all of them survived the trip to school. To Molly's amazement, upon being placed in the box, the ants refused to follow the maze walls. Instead, they climbed them. A good many escaped to the project on the neighboring table, a collection of various liquids that the student was claiming could melt cotton candy quicker than human saliva could."

The crowd is really laughing now. Even my parents are smiling a little.

"Within a minute, there wasn't a single ant left on the top of Molly's desk. I told her not to feel bad about her project, to which she replied, 'Oh, I don't. I think the results affirm my theory. Ants are the only animal smart enough to escape the maze.'"

People continue to laugh. The only person I can see who isn't laughing is that stupid mortuary worker standing beside my casket. But I guess that makes sense. To work with dead bodies, you must have a totally different sense of humor from the rest of humanity.

"In closing, I want to say that I remember Molly Weller as a unique thinker. I was saddened to hear about her tragic death. The young should never die. But Molly and her sense of humor are not lost; they are not gone. I believe she can be with us always, as long as we keep her in our thoughts. In that way, she will live on. Molly herself has escaped the maze."

The laughter has given way to sobs. I look at my parents.

I look at Henry. It's so clear now. I'd been worried about my fate, but what you love *is* your fate. I wish I could have known that before I invited Hilda to appear. Why am I such a slow learner? Wherever she is in the room, she's doing an excellent job of blending in. Mrs. Oswald walks to her chair. I watch as my aunt Claire gets up to give a speech. She grabs on to the podium with both hands. Then her nerves get the better of her, and out of nowhere she starts to giggle. Her face turns red.

"I'm sorry," she says, as she turns her head to one side.

I think people assume that she's breaking down, not cracking up. I move toward her. Maybe my soul can bring her back to her senses. If I stand next to her, at least I'll be able to read her speech. It may be the only way I'll get to know what it says.

As I move out of the corner, I notice that the slant of light on the floor next to Aunt Claire is growing. It's the door. Oh my god. I rush toward it. I stand right in front of it. This is going to be so easy. My portal is right here. My grandmother stands up and tries to hand Aunt Claire a glass of water.

That's when I realize that I may be doomed. Climbing the two shallow stairs that lead to the speaking platform, my grandmother trips and slams right into the mortuary worker. But somehow, she doesn't make contact. She falls through him and lands on top of my casket. My casket is on wheels and rolls a little bit. My grandmother spills the water all over the flowers. That's not so bad. It will keep them alive longer.

"No," I tell Hilda. She looks at me and winks. Then hovers next to my grandma.

For some reason, she continues to pretend not to be Hilda. Clearly, the worker isn't a flesh-and-blood person; he's a soul.

"This is my door," I say.

Hilda doesn't respond. She keeps standing beside my casket, in the guise of mortuary worker. I stay where I am. It's exactly like waiting for an elevator to arrive. The door is almost fully outlined now. I'm waiting to see the knob. Aunt Claire has helped my grandma back to her seat and gathered her thoughts.

"When I think of Molly, I'm struck by the fact that she had her whole life ahead of her," Aunt Claire says to the mourners.

Where is the doorknob?

"I think you're standing on the wrong side," the mortuary worker (aka Hilda) says.

"Nice try, Hilda."

Like I'm going to fall for that.

"Who's Hilda? I'm your grandpa Jean. I'm going to help you cross."

A gray-haired woman runs through Aunt Claire. It's Mr. Dunkley's wife. What is she doing? Now she's standing on the other side of the door.

"Hurry, Molly," my grandpa yells.

I race around the door. Does Mr. Dunkley even have a wife? It's Hilda, and she has her arm outstretched and is almost touching the knob.

"This is my destiny," I yell. "It's meant for me."

"Not if I get there first," Hilda says. "I'm sick of being uncrossed."

She tries to shove me, but her arms pass through me. I'm one hundred percent soul. But when I push Hilda's shoulder, she tumbles. I've made contact with the small amount of her that she's retrained to be a body. She falls on the floor, her legs akimbo beneath my casket.

"Grandpa, hold her."

"I've never been to a funeral where I've had to do this," he says.

He grabs her by the foot.

"Let go!" Hilda cries.

"Molly Weller knew who she was and where she was going," Aunt Claire says. "I'm sure of that."

I reach out and touch the door. My grandfather, whom I've never met until this awkward moment, takes my hand. But I can't cross yet. Not without looking at everyone I love one final time. The last person I glimpse is Henry. Sad, geeky, talented Henry. I will miss that future. So much.

"You lead," my grandpa says. "That's how it's done."

Behind us, Hilda is wailing about how unfair things are, about how she deserves to finally cross.

"It's my turn!" she hollers. "My turn!"

I pull open the door and walk toward a bright light. I assume my grandpa is behind me. But as I walk toward this clean nothingness, I feel myself growing heavy. It's similar to the sensation of being alive.

"Where are we going?" I ask.

But nobody is with me anymore. Not my parents, the twins, my friends, Henry. Oh, Henry. I'm walking alone. My mind is spinning with possibilities. What if this is just a dream? What if I've been in a coma? Or what if I'm headed to Heaven?

All three things feel equally possible.

The only thing I'm certain of is that I'm walking toward my destiny. That's what I know for sure. Where am I going? How will I know when I get there? In a strange way, this moment is a lot like life. It's what I was doing every day before my accident.

I keep stepping forward, a little uncertain, moving toward something unknown. I'm almost excited. The white world around me starts turning faster and faster, and I'm thrilled. There's light. And more light. How will I know when I've arrived? A pin pricks me. I close my eyes. I open them. I am here. But where? I don't know. But I am here. I am. I feel lucky. I feel happy. I feel like I'm alive.

Acknowledgments

could not have finished this book without the support of several friends. Thank you, Stacey Kade, Cory Grimminck, Regina Marler, Joen Madonna, Ulla Frederiksen, Kristin Scheel, and Brian Evenson. You improve everything. I also need to thank Emily Schultz, who supported this book from the very beginning. I owe you. There were also several people who provided timely inspiration. Thanks to Tobias Wolff for giving me a great jazz CD. And thanks to Patrick Wolff for thoroughly answering my many saxophone questions.

And thank you to all the hardworking and wonderful people at Disney-Hyperion. Thank you, Catherine Onder, my super-smart editor, for making this book the best version of itself. And thank you, Jennifer Corcoran and Hallie Patterson, for your support and kindness and problem-solving abilities. And thanks to Christian Trimmer, Dina Sherman, Nellie Kurtzman, and Stephanie Lurie for all the support behind the scenes. And lastly, I want to thank Hayley Wagreich, for catching everything I missed. I am incredibly happy this book found such a wonderful home.